INNOVATIONS

SPACE

Ron Miller

Twenty-First Century Books

Minneapolis

To Oliver Rin Kutschinski

Twenty-First Century Books
A division of Lerner Publishing Group, Inc.
241 First Avenue North
Minneapolis, MN 55401 U.S.A.

Website address: www.lernerbooks.com

Library of Congress Cataloging-in-Publication Data

Miller, Ron, 1947–
    Robot explorers / by Ron Miller.
        p.   cm. — (Space innovations)
    Includes bibliographical references and index.
    ISBN 978-0-8225-7152-0 (lib. bdg. : alk. paper)
    1. Space probes—Juvenile literature. 2. Space robotics—Juvenile literature.
    I. Title.
    TL795.3.M55 2008
    629.43'54—dc22   2007002864

Manufactured in the United States of America
1 2 3 4 5 6 – DP – 13 12 11 10 09 08

CONTENTS

Human curiosity about the world has led people to poke into every corner of this planet. Explorers have reached the tops of the highest mountains and plumbed the farthest depths of the oceans. People have crawled into caverns hundreds of feet below Earth's surface and climbed into the craters of active volcanoes. Humans have even explored regions beyond Earth's atmosphere. But what if an environment is so hostile that no matter how well protected, a human being could never survive it? Or what if someplace is so hard to get to that it would cost many billions of dollars for a human to get there?

Many of the other worlds in our solar system are not nearly as inviting to humans as Earth. Io, one of the big moons of Jupiter, would be one of the most fascinating worlds in the entire solar system to visit. It has a brilliantly colored landscape, lakes of molten sulfur, and giant volcanoes. But it lies within a belt of intense radiation surrounding Jupiter. The radiation would quickly microwave any visiting astronauts.

What if it's possible to get some idea of what these places are like without sending astronauts? Robots can do a lot of the exploring for us and are much cheaper to send to a planet or a moon than a human being. Robots don't need food, oxygen, life-support systems, and all the other baggage human explorers require. Robots are safer too. If a robot is lost, scientists can always build another one.

The more scientists know about a place before sending astronauts, the safer the astronauts will be. This book is about how robots have helped humans explore the solar system, the amazing discoveries they have made, and some of the incredible things they may help us do in the future.

One of the most successful of all robotic missions to Mars has been the two rovers that have been exploring the Martian surface for years beyond their planned ninety-day mission. Among their many discoveries is proof that large bodies of water existed on Mars in the past.

1

In 1610 Italian scientist Galileo Galilei began using a new invention called the telescope. He turned it toward the night sky. He discovered that the Moon was a world not unlike our own, with mountains, valleys, and plains. He also learned that the planets are more than just bright stars. They are worlds too. From that moment, humans started dreaming about visiting these places, but they had no practical way of doing it.

People came up with all sorts of imaginary ways to travel into space—from balloons to giant cannons. But it turned out that the answer lay in one of humankind's oldest inventions— one that was already more than six hundred years old when Galileo made his discovery.

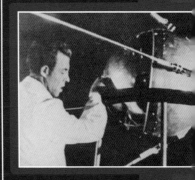

Top: A nineteenth-century watercolor shows ancient Chinese rocket makers at work. *Center:* U.S. physicist Robert Goddard took rocket technology in a whole new direction in the late 1920s. *Bottom:* The Soviets launched *Sputnik I* into Earth's orbit in 1957, beating the efforts of the United States by almost four months. The space race was on.

This 1952 watercolor painting by Jack Coggins shows the first recorded use of rockets in warfare. It occurred in A.D. 1232 at the Battle of Kai-fung-fu. The city was under siege by the Mongols, who were repulsed when the Chinese used rockets against them.

THE ROCKET

The ancient Chinese invented the rocket about one thousand years ago. They first used the rocket in festivals and celebrations—like modern Fourth of July fireworks. However, the military quickly adopted the rocket as a weapon. As a weapon, the rocket was not a full success. By the nineteenth century, advances in the art of cannon making had relegated the rocket to the status of a minor amusement. Few people thought that the rocket might be applied to transportation, let alone flight into space.

In 1929 U.S. physicist Robert Goddard invented a new type of rocket. Instead of being powered by gunpowder, it was powered by liquid fuels. This new type of rocket was much more powerful and reliable than the one the Chinese had invented.

Improvements in liquid-fueled rockets drew the attention of the

The German liquid-fuel V-2 rocket takes off *(above)* during World War II (1939–1945). The technology developed to propel missiles and rockets led to future space exploration and advancements in the understanding of the solar system.

German military, which invested heavily in their development. By the end of World War II (1939–1945), liquid-fuel rockets had grown to immense sizes. The largest gunpowder rockets of the nineteenth century were only a few feet long and weighed perhaps 100 pounds (45 kilograms). But the giant German V-2 rocket of World War II was 46 feet (14 meters) tall and weighed 27,576 pounds (12,508 kg). It could reach altitudes of nearly 100 miles (160 kilometers)—the very fringe of outer space.

Many scientists—including German engineer Wernher von Braun, who helped develop the V-2 rocket—believed that the giant missile held the key to future space travel. But few countries had any interest in paying for space travel at that time.

THE RACE BEGINS

While the United States and the Soviet Union had been allies in World War II, they became bitter rivals afterward. These two nations began developing nuclear weapons such as the atomic bomb and the hydrogen bomb. Both countries also began looking at other military uses for rockets. They soon realized that rockets were the ideal device for sending nuclear weapons to their targets. Rockets could carry heavy loads and travel thousands of miles at extremely high speeds, many times faster than any aircraft.

Scientists also realized that such giant rockets would be capable of boosting satellites into orbit around Earth. These satellites could carry spy equipment such as powerful cameras or even atomic bombs that could be dropped from space. The governments of the United States and the Soviet Union finally had a compelling reason to invest in space travel.

Another compelling reason emerged. The first country to reach outer space would gain great prestige. The accomplishment would be a source of immense national pride. This attitude sparked a space race between the United States and the Soviet Union that began with the launch of the first Earth satellites in the 1950s.

The big military rockets were perfect for boosting satellites into orbit. The first artificial Earth satellites—the Soviet Union's *Sputnik 1* in 1957 and the U.S. *Explorer 1* in 1958—were both launched by rockets originally designed to deliver nuclear weapons.

The governments of the Soviet Union and the United States didn't want the space race to seem like a race for military supremacy, however. Neither country wanted to appear as a potential aggressor. Although the two countries were enemies, they were not at war with each other and preferred to keep it that way. Fortunately, scientists had plenty of other valid reasons to travel into space. No one knew anything about the conditions beyond Earth's atmosphere. In fact, scientists didn't even know for sure if humans would be able to survive traveling in space. The only way to safely explore space was to send automatic—robotic—instruments.

2

After the United States and the Soviet Union had successfully placed the first satellites in orbit around Earth, exploring the Moon became their next goal. The first probes to the Moon had the simplest mission: could someone *get* there. The United States made the first attempt. The U.S. Army and U.S. Air Force launched the Pioneer lunar probes in August, October, and December of 1958. The probes failed to achieve escape velocity—the speed necessary to escape the pull of Earth's gravity (about 7 miles [11.3 km] per second)—and fell back to Earth. All wasn't a total loss, though. The probes reached high enough altitudes—up to 70,700 miles (113,777 km)—to return valuable information about the Van Allen radiation belts that circle Earth. The Van Allen belts are doughnut-shaped regions of high radiation that present a danger to human spaceflight.

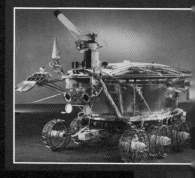

Top: This image of the Moon's Tycho crater is the combined result of many images taken by the Lunar Orbiters. *Center:* The lunar lander *Surveyor 3* was still on the Moon in November 1969 when *Apollo 12* landed there. The astronauts brought back parts of the lander for study. *Bottom: Lunokhod 1*, the first wheeled space vehicle, influenced later land rover designs.

On September 12, 1959, the Soviets launched *Luna 2*. (The previous attempt, *Luna 1*, had failed to reach its target.) When the 860-pound (390 kg) spacecraft hit the Moon, it became the first human-made object to ever touch another world—even if its only accomplishment was to blast a small crater in it.

The Soviet Union launched *Luna 3* in October 1959. Its mission was to swing around the Moon. Passing within 4,900 miles (7,890 km) of the surface, *Luna 3* returned the first-ever pictures of the lunar farside. Because the Moon rotates in the same time it takes to make one revolution around Earth, people on Earth can see only one side of the Moon. Before *Luna 3* circled the Moon, no human being had ever seen the side facing away from Earth.

 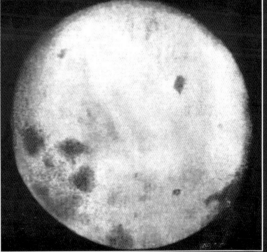

The Soviets displayed the *Luna 3* probe *(left)* before its launch to the Moon. The dark panels near the top of the probe are solar cells that generate electricity. *Luna 3* sent back the first photo ever taken of the far side of the Moon *(right)*. Many U.S. scientists were skeptical, thinking that the Soviets might have faked the image in order to beat the United States to this accomplishment. One of the reasons for this skepticism is the lack of detail in the photo. However, the later U.S. Lunar Orbiter probes took photos confirming some of the features.

TOUCHING THE MOON

The first human contact with the Moon occurred in 1946 when the U.S. Army's Project Diana sent a radar signal into space. (Diana was the Roman goddess of the Moon.) A few minutes later, the army detected a return signal as the radar waves bounced off the Moon. This experiment had little value for discovering anything about the Moon. It did, however, help scientists develop the technology to detect very weak signals coming from great distances. This technology was essential for communicating with spacecraft as they began traveling ever farther from Earth.

The spacecraft photographed about 70 percent of the farside. About 30 percent of the photos showed features on the nearside. The recognizable features helped astronomers orient the images in relation to known craters, mare (flat, gray lava plains), and mountains. Although the image quality was poor, scientists found the photos very exciting. Many of the features on the farside of the Moon have Russian names because the Soviets were the first to take photos of them.

THE RANGERS

The Soviet successes in space gave the U.S. lunar exploration program a new urgency. In 1958 the United States created a new government agency: the National Aeronautics and Space Administration (NASA). Before then the U.S. military, which owned big booster rockets, conducted satellite launches. But NASA, as a civilian (nonmilitary) agency, developed its own boosters exclusively for space exploration. This change helped to remove any hint that the U.S. space effort was for military purposes.

On May 25, 1961, President John F. Kennedy made a bold speech to the U.S. Congress. He said, "I believe that this nation should commit itself to achieving the goal before the decade is out of landing a man on the Moon and returning him safely to Earth." Kennedy's announcement put a hard deadline on what had originally been a long-range plan to explore the Moon.

Wernher von Braun, like many other scientists, had imagined a step-by-step program in which satellites would be followed by space-craft carrying human beings. Next would come a space station, which would be followed by astronauts orbiting the Moon and, finally, land-ing on it. This careful approach would have taken a long time, but before 1961, NASA had been in no particular hurry. Kennedy's plans gave rocket engineers less than nine years to achieve a goal they thought would take twenty or more.

The United States made eleven more attempts to reach the Moon between 1958 and 1964. The spacecraft on these missions all failed for one reason or another. Although pure scientific research was part of the mission of the lunar probes, the probes also had to gather information relevant to the coming astronaut landings. Scientists needed to answer a lot of questions. What was the environ-ment of the Moon like? Exactly what was its surface like? Where were the best places to land? Where were the safest? All of these questions and more needed to be answered before a human being could land on the Moon.

Finally, in July 1964, *Ranger 7* plummeted to the Moon's sur-face, snapping photos the entire time. NASA designed the Ranger series of spacecraft to take close-up photos of the lunar surface. The solar-powered spacecraft carried six television cameras. The cam-eras began filming about fifteen to twenty minutes before impact. In that time, the probe fell toward the Moon at a speed of 5,999 miles per hour (9,654 km/h). Each minute, the probe sent back three hun-dred pictures. Those pictures provided views of the Moon nearly a

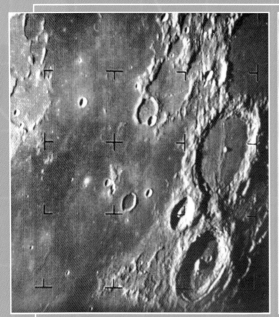 

A Ranger probe took this photo *(left)* as it dropped toward the Moon, about fifteen minutes before impact. *Ranger 7* took its last photo *(right)* as it plummeted into the Moon, about one second before impact. The Ranger images surprised scientists by revealing a surface much more heavily cratered than expected. No matter how close any of the Rangers got, the photos always showed craters. They proved that landing a person on the Moon was not going to be as easy as scientists hoped.

thousand times better than any that scientists could obtain from Earth. *Ranger 7* took 4,306 high-resolution images in all. Seven months later, *Ranger 8* did even better, returning 7,137 pictures before impacting in Mare Tranquillitatis—one of the broad, flat ancient lava plains on the Moon.

In all, the Ranger series returned more than seventeen thousand photos. The closest snapshot was taken from a distance of only 1,575 feet (480 m), revealing details at a resolution two thousand times greater than any Earth-based telescope. Scientists could see features as small as 15 inches (38 centimeters) wide. (By contrast, Earth-based telescopes can see only details roughly 0.25 mile [about 0.5 km] across.) Scientists discovered that the Moon has craters of all sizes. No matter how close the probe got, all the photos showed craters.

THE LUNAR ORBITER AND SURVEYOR SERIES

Only three of the seven Ranger probes NASA sent to the Moon successfully returned images. In the Lunar Orbiter program that followed, all five spacecraft were successful. The Orbiters' main objective was to discover potential landing sites for the upcoming Apollo lunar landing program. Between August 1966 and August 1967, the Lunar Orbiters photographed 99.5 percent of the Moon's surface, including the farside and the south pole. One of the Lunar Orbiters even caught Earth hovering above the lunar horizon. This was the first photo of Earth as seen from the Moon.

The Orbiters also made many important scientific discoveries. For instance, variations in their orbits revealed huge concentrations of mass (material) under the lunar lava plains. Scientists suspect that huge asteroids created these plains. The mass concentrations—called mascons—might be remnants of the asteroids. Scientists discovered twelve mascons on the nearside alone.

Lunar Orbiter 1 took this historic photo in 1966, the first ever to show Earth from the Moon—236,000 miles (380,000 km) away.

MAPPING THE MOON

Before the advent of space travel, scientists could only map the Moon by observing it through telescopes based on Earth. Scientists drew these early maps by hand. At the end of the nineteenth century and the first half of the twentieth century, high-resolution telescopic photographs aided lunar mapmakers.

Mapmakers had two big problems, though. First, only one side of the Moon faces Earth. Mapmakers had no way to see and map the other side. Second, the Moon is a sphere, so features that are near the edge of the Moon are severely distorted.

Plans to land humans on the Moon created a need for exstremely detailed, accurate maps. These required much more detail than humans could observe from Earth. Spacecraft flying near the Moon provided this crucial information. The Lunar Orbiter spacecraft in the 1960s allowed scientists to create the first highly detailed maps of the Moon, which included features that were either very difficult or impossible to see from Earth.

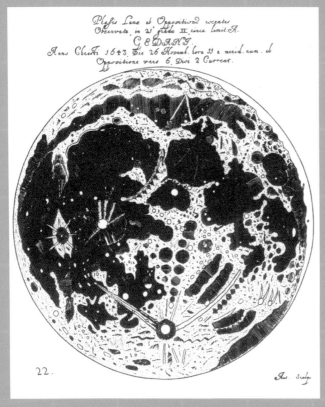

This map drawn by German-Polish astronomer Johannes Hevel in 1647 was one of the first attempts to accurately chart the Moon.

Scientists combined many Lunar Orbiter images to create this view of the lunar crater Tycho. The Lunar Orbiters took their photos on long strips of film, which were then scanned and broadcast back to Earth. These strips were then assembled side by side to create the finished photo.

NASA didn't want the five orbiters to continue circling the Moon when their missions were completed. Their orbits would have caused problems for the astronauts who would be arriving soon. Eventually, NASA made all the Lunar Orbiters crash into the Moon.

After the Orbiters came the Surveyor series. U.S. scientists designed the Surveyors to land on the Moon. They provided the final information about conditions on the Moon prior to manned landings. The Surveyor spacecraft took photos and analyzed soil samples.

The Soviets had already reached this stage of lunar exploration. The Soviet *Luna 9* made the first successful soft landing on the Moon in January 1966. It sent back the first photos taken on the surfaces of the Moon. For four days, it also sent data about radiation on the surface. Most of the surface radiation comes from the Sun. Earth's atmosphere shields us from this harmful radiation, but the Moon has no atmosphere. If the radiation levels on the Moon were too high, astronauts walking on the surface could be harmed. Fortunately, it turned out that the radiation levels were low enough for astronauts to withstand.

NASA launched *Surveyor 1* in May 1966. It made a successful landing. *Surveyor 1* sent 237 photos of the lunar surface back to Earth. *Surveyors* 2 and 4 crashed while trying to land, but *Surveyors* 3, 5, 6, and 7 made it. All took thousands of photos of their landing sites. The final three landers also collected soil samples and analyzed them.

All the Surveyors have a similar basic design. Three legs with landing pads supported a triangular base of metal tubes. The base held scientific instruments and the fuel, motors, and controls needed for landing. It also had the antennae needed for communication with Earth. A tripod supported a camera, and a tall mast held up a pair of solar panels.

In 1966 *Surveyor 1* returned some of the first photos ever taken from the surface of the Moon.

Surveyor 5 took this photo of one of its own landing pads, showing the soft, dusty surface of the Moon. The photo proved—much to the relief of the scientists planning the first manned mission to the Moon—that the surface could safely support a lander and astronauts.

The last three Surveyors had a movable arm with a small scoop at one end. With this, the probe could scrape at the nearby soil, determine its consistency, and carry samples back to the miniature chemical analyzer on board. Scientists planning future manned missions to the Moon needed to know what the surface was like. A hard crust would present no problem, but a lander might sink if the surface turned out to be covered with a thick layer of dust. Scientists discovered that while the surface had a lot of dust, it was only a few inches deep, with a hard rocky layer just beneath.

GREAT ACHIEVEMENTS

So far, neither the Soviet Union nor the United States had won the space race. Every achievement made by either nation was a great step forward in the exploration of space. Nevertheless, the spectacular firsts always made the headlines. But when *Apollo 11* landed on the Moon on

July 20, 1969, many people around the world considered the United States the clear winner.

Soon after, *Apollo 12* astronauts Alan Bean and Pete Conrad set down their spacecraft about 197 feet (60 m) from the *Surveyor 3* that had landed there two years earlier. After photographing the lander, the crew retrieved several pieces of it, including the TV camera and its cables, the sample scoop, and some aluminum tubing. They brought these pieces back to Earth. Scientists studied them to determine how the lunar environment had affected them.

The Soviet space program was not as successful with its lunar missions in the late 1960s. Only a handful of Soviet lunar probes completed their missions. One mission, however, was a resounding

The *Apollo 12* lunar module *(in the distance)* set down near the *Surveyor 3* lander. The Apollo astronauts were able to remove and return pieces of *Surveyor 3* to Earth. Scientists were anxious to see how different materials reacted to being in space for so many years.

In 1970 the Soviet *Luna 16* lander *(right)* took samples of the lunar surface and returned them to Earth for study. It was the first time scientists examined actual specimens of the Moon's soil.

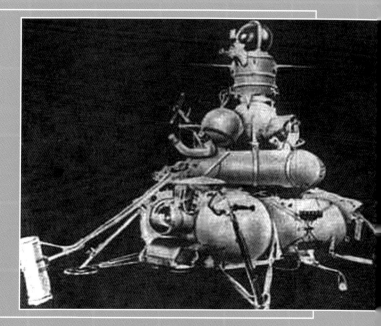

success. The *Luna 16* lander made a safe landing on the Moon in September 1970. It had an arm with a drill attached. This arm could be lowered to the ground, where the drill bored into the surface, gathering samples. The arm then raised the hollow drill and its enclosed samples to a small capsule sitting on the very top of the lander. The arm transferred the soil samples to the capsule, which had a rocket booster attached. The capsule was then launched back to Earth, where the Soviets recovered it. Although the Soviets achieved the first automatic retrieval of a lunar soil sample, the general public didn't notice its historic significance. The U.S. Apollo program overshadowed this accomplishment.

The next Luna lander, *Luna 17*, contained a major surprise for U.S. scientists: an eight-wheeled lunar rover. *Lunokhod 1* was a 200-pound (91 kg) solar-powered vehicle that very much resembled a washtub on wheels. It was a miniature rolling laboratory equipped with television cameras, soil probes, and analyzers. For ten and a half months, it wandered a total distance of 34,588 feet (10,542 m) over the lunar surface, stopping often to test the soil. *Lunokhod 1* had a

On November 17, 1970, the Soviet's *Lunokhod 1* rover was the first wheeled vehicle to explore another world.

great influence over the design of future rovers, including those that will be exploring Mars in the twenty-first century.

RETURN TO THE MOON

After the Apollo missions, scientists looked elsewhere in the solar system for places to investigate. More than twenty years passed before scientists resumed exploring the Moon. In recent years, interest in the Moon has reawakened, with several new missions making some surprising discoveries.

For its missions in the early twenty-first century, NASA implemented a "faster, cheaper, better" approach to the spacecraft construction and mission planning. The *Clementine* spacecraft went from conceptual design to launch in only twenty-two months and at a cost of just $80 million. This was the first time NASA used this approach in a space program. The costs of previous deep space missions had been significantly higher and took a great deal more time to develop.

NASA launched *Clementine* on January 25, 1994. Officially known as the Deep Space Program Science Experiment (DSPSE), its mission involved testing lightweight miniature sensors and advanced spacecraft components that future interplanetary probes would use. *Clementine*'s primary task was to create a detailed map of the Moon. *Clementine* succeeded beyond all expectations. Its lunar map is the most detailed ever made.

Between February 26 and April 22, 1994, *Clementine* sent more than 1.8 million digital images of the Moon back to Earth. NASA posted these images on the Internet so the general public could see them. The scientists examining the data from *Clementine* made a major scientific discovery. They found the possibility of ice within the Moon's craters near the south pole, where the craters have been permanently shaded from the Sun's rays.

NASA's *Lunar Prospector* confirmed this discovery in early 1998. The *Lunar Prospector* was a nineteen-month mission designed for a low polar orbit investigation of the Moon. It included measurements of magnetic and gravity fields and mapping of surface composition and possible polar ice deposits. The search for water ice was a spectacular success. *Prospector* discovered ice in deep craters at both the north and south poles of the Moon.

The polar ice deposits were an important find for scientists who had been interested in establishing a permanent human base on the Moon. Not only is a source of water important, but water can be broken down into hydrogen and oxygen. Hydrogen is a main source of energy, and oxygen is necessary to human life. The water probably

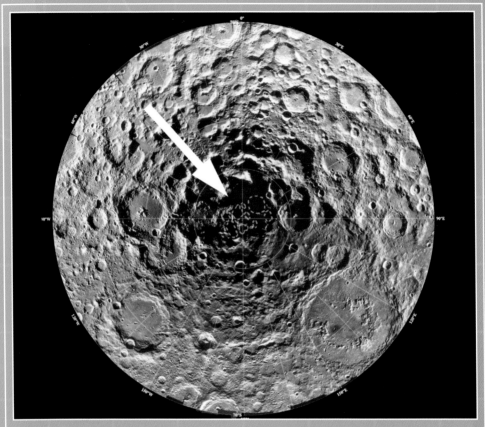

The *Clementine* orbiter created this image of the Moon's south pole. The areas indicated in blue are regions where *Clementine* found deposits of ice in the bottoms of craters permanently shaded from the Sun.

arrived when comets—which are composed mostly of water ice—crashed into the Moon. Little or no sunlight penetrates into the depths of many of the craters closest to the south pole. So the ice did not boil away. Anywhere else on the Moon, water would have been exposed to the heat of the Sun.

The *Lunar Prospector* was also supposed to study lunar outgassing (the release of gases from soil or crust of a moon or planet). Scientists had long suspected that various gases periodically escaped from deep within the Moon's crust. Unfortunately, the instrument designed to detect these gases was damaged during takeoff, and the experiment had to be abandoned. The mission ended July 31,

1999, when the orbiter was deliberately crashed into a crater near the lunar south pole in an attempt to detect the presence of water. Scientists hoped that the impact would liberate water vapor from the ice deposits in the crater and that the plume—a cloud of water vapor—would be detectable from Earth. Unfortunately, scientists did not observe a cloud.

INTERNATIONAL SPACE EXPLORATION

The United States and the Soviet Union (which broke apart into Russia and fourteen other republics in 1991) aren't the only countries that have been interested in exploring the Moon. Japanese scientists and engineers have long been interested in the possibilities of lunar exploration. In 1990 Japan's Institute of Space and Astronautical Science (ISAS) launched a scientific satellite named *Hiten*. *Hiten*'s goal was to establish the technologies that would be needed for future lunar and planetary exploration projects. *Hiten* completed its mission successfully.

In July 1994, Japan's Space Activities Commission (SAC) developed a program called Long-term Vision, declaring the Moon as one of the main targets for national space development. This announcement inspired the SELENE Project (SELenological and ENgineering Explorer Project—Selene was also the name of the Greek goddess of the Moon). The SELENE Project is a joint mission of the National Space Development Agency of Japan and the Institute of Space and Astronautical Science. (Both organizations are part of the Japanese Aerospace Exploration Agency—JAXA.) Although not scheduled for launch yet, the SELENE Project has been making steady progress.

VENUS

3

Ever since Galileo Galilei first observed Venus with a telescope in 1610, the planet has

been one of the most mysterious worlds in the solar system. Venus is almost exactly the same size and mass as Earth. It resembles our own planet so closely that it has been called Earth's twin sister. But Venus's surface is veiled behind a dense, impenetrable layer of clouds.

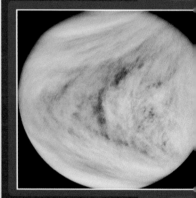

Until the first probes flew past the planet in the 1960s, scientists could only guess what lay beneath the clouds. Some scientists thought it might have a prehistoric world, much like Earth many millions of years ago, with lush rain forests and strange life-forms. Some thought that Venus might be covered by a vast, worldwide ocean. Others suggested that Venus might be a scorched, desertlike world. No one even knew for sure how fast Venus rotated on its axis, because they couldn't see the surface.

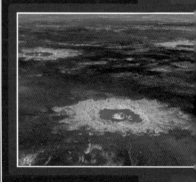

Top: A mock-up of a Soviet Venera lander stands in a museum in Moscow, Russia. *Center:* A photo of Venus shrouded by clouds was taken by *Pioneer-Venus 1. Bottom:* A computer reconstruction of the surface of Venus was created by *Magellan* radar data.

A DIFFICULT TARGET

Sending a probe to Venus was much more difficult than sending one to the Moon. At its closest, Venus is a hundred times farther away from Earth than the Moon is. Scientists needed a much bigger, more powerful rocket to send a probe that far. The Soviet Union developed a rocket powerful enough in 1964 with its A-2-e booster. Almost immediately, the Soviet Union began launching probes to both Venus and Mars. And these probes almost immediately ran into trouble. The Soviet Union tried to reach Venus and Mars seventeen times between 1960 and 1967. Every probe failed. Some of the probes never left Earth. Others reached their goal but failed to return any data.

The United States suffered its share of disappointments too, but it didn't have to wait seven years for its first success. The second interplanetary probe NASA launched, *Mariner 2*, made a flyby (flying close enough to observe without orbiting or landing) of Venus in 1962. *Mariner 2* discovered that Venus had an extremely dense atmosphere and hot surface. Temperatures on the planet are

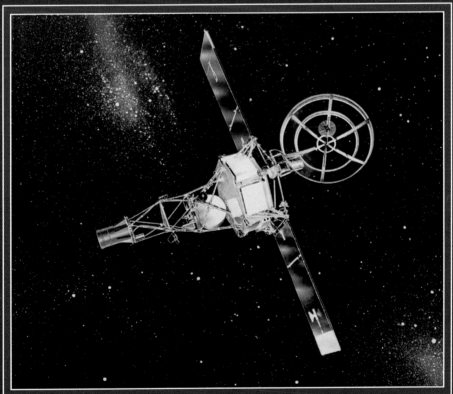

An artist's impression shows *Mariner 2* making a flyby of Venus in 1962.

GETTING FROM HERE TO THERE

It might seem that the simplest way to travel from planet to planet would be to just get in a rocket and blast directly from one place to another. But since Earth is already moving, the rocket would first have to counter Earth's speed and direction when leaving its orbit (the path of a planet around the Sun) and then match the speed and direction of its destination. This would require a lot of fuel. A simpler way to travel from one planet to another is to use a Hohmann orbit. It is named for Walter Hohmann, the German mathematician who first suggested it in 1925. Traveling along a Hohmann orbit takes much longer than going in a straight line from planet to planet, but this type of orbit uses energy much more efficiently.

When planning a trip into space, scientists want to choose a trajectory (path) that makes the most efficient use of the fuel that the spacecraft carries. Fuel is expensive primarily because of the weight it adds to the spacecraft. The heavier a rocket is, the more fuel it needs to burn to get to its destination. The more fuel the rocket needs, the heavier it is.

Hohmann came up with a way for a rocket to travel through space by taking advantage of a planet's speed and direction as it orbits around the Sun. Instead of a rocket having to burn its own energy to counteract the effects of planetary motions—that is, to travel in a different direction from the rotation of the planet around the Sun—a rocket would hitch a ride in a planet's orbit and would fire its engines as necessary to change its trajectory enough to enter another planet's orbit.

For example, to launch a spacecraft from Earth to an outer planet (one farther away from the Sun than Earth), such as Mars, first consider that Earth, and therefore the spacecraft on Earth, is in orbit. The spaceship needs to expend only enough energy to put it into a new orbit. The spacecraft fires its rockets to lift off the launchpad and rise above Earth's atmosphere.

greater than that of molten lead: 750°F (400°C). Scientists no longer had any hope of finding life on that world.

The Soviets scored the next success. *Venera 4* made an entry into Venus's atmosphere in 1967. *Venera 4* transmitted data back to

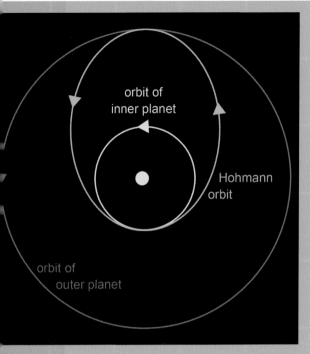

orbit of
inner planet

Hohmann
orbit

orbit of
outer planet

A Hohmann orbit (green line) is the most efficient way to travel from planet to planet. To travel from an outer planet (red) to an inner planet (yellow), a spacecraft must be launched into an elliptical orbit that intersects both the inner and outer orbits. The same procedure is used to travel from an inner planet to an outer one. The only difference is that a decrease in orbital speed is needed to travel from an outer planet to an inner planet. Conversely, an increase in orbital speed is needed to travel from an inner planet to an outer one.

Then it uses its rocket to accelerate (speed up) in the direction of Earth's orbit around the Sun. This acceleration will change the spacecraft's trajectory, allowing it to fly in a new, larger orbit. The spacecraft's new orbit will then intersect the orbit of its destination planet, Mars. The spaceship then fires its rockets for the second time, in the reverse direction to slow it down in its approach to Mars. In between these two rocket bursts, the spaceship coasts, using no fuel at all.

The use of a Hohmann orbit to travel from planet to planet requires precise timing. The spacecraft has to arrive at the orbit of its destination planet at exactly the same time the planet arrives at that same point. If it arrives too early or too late, the planet won't be there. An astronaut who plans to use a Hohmann orbit must leave Earth at a very precise time—usually within a few days or a few weeks at most— to arrive at their destination on time. This exact departure time is called the launch window.

Earth while it descended to within 16 miles (25 km) of the scorching surface. The Soviets launched the next successful Venus probe in 1970 with *Venera 7*. It survived entry into Venus's atmosphere and touched down on the surface. *Venera 7* was the first human-made

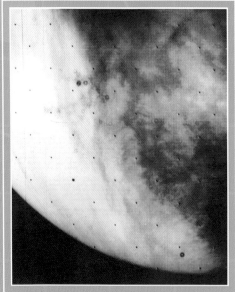

This is one of the first images of Venus sent back by *Mariner 10*, which photographed the planet as it passed by on its way to Mercury. *Mariner 10* was the first spacecraft to ever visit more than one planet.

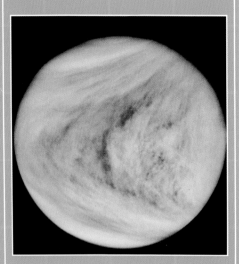

An image of the planet Venus taken by *Pioneer-Venus 1* shows that the surface of the planet is hidden beneath a dense layer of clouds rich in sulfuric acid.

object to ever land on the surface of another planet.

The United States did not have another successful Venus mission until *Mariner 10* in 1973. That spacecraft took the first television images of Venus while on its way to an encounter with the planet Mercury. Two years later, the Soviets had a double victory when they landed not one but two probes on the surface of Venus. Both transmitted data back to Earth. But one of the probes sent the first images of the surface of Venus as well, revealing rocks that looked like solidified lava.

A great number of spacecraft reached Venus in the following decade and a half. The United States launched *Pioneer-Venus 1* and *2* in 1978. *Pioneer-Venus 1* first orbited the planet, sending back data. *Pioneer-Venus 2* released entry probes that returned data from the surface.

The Soviets countered with *Venera 11, 12, 13,* and *14,* which were all flyby probes that

This photo *(above)* taken by the Soviet *Venera 14* lander is the only color image of the surface of Venus. *Venera 14* took this photo *(right)* of the surface of Venus. Any probe that lands on the surface of Venus only lasts for a few minutes. It is quickly destroyed by the hostile conditions—extreme heat, sulfuric acid rain, and crushing atmospheric pressure.

released landers as they passed by the planet. All of them transmitted data about surface conditions as well as photos of the landing sites, including the first color pictures taken of Venus's surface. *Venera 15* and *16* only orbited Venus. The Soviet *Vega 1* and *2* sent landers to the surface and also released French-made atmospheric balloon probes. The balloon probes drifted rapidly through Venus's sky, driven by the planet's hurricane-force winds, while sending data back to Earth.

MAGELLAN

Perhaps one of the most successful and important of all the probes sent to Venus was the *Magellan* orbiter, which NASA launched in 1989. NASA named *Magellan* after the sixteenth-century Portuguese explorer Ferdinand Magellan. He initiated the expedition that was the first to sail entirely around the world.

Magellan was the first interplanetary spacecraft to be launched by a space shuttle. The shuttle *Atlantis* carried *Magellan* into low Earth orbit, where it was released from the shuttle's cargo bay. A rocket motor then fired, sending *Magellan* on a fifteen-month cruise into the inner solar system. After looping around the Sun one and a half times, the spacecraft finally arrived at Venus on August 10, 1990. Another rocket motor then fired, placing *Magellan* in orbit around the planet.

Magellan's orbit was polar, meaning that the spacecraft passed over Venus's north and south poles during every three-hour-fifteen-minute orbit. The result was that as the planet slowly rotated beneath the spacecraft, *Magellan* eventually passed over every square mile of its surface. Although Venus's dense clouds cannot be penetrated by visible light, other wavelengths, such as radar, can go through them. By measuring the strength of the signal bouncing back from the surface, maps can be created. *Magellan* carried out a radar-mapping mission until 1994.

Venus rotates once every 243 Earth days, and *Magellan* gathered photographs of the entire planet during that time.

THE PLANETS OF THE SOLAR SYSTEM

Planet	Mercury	Venus	Earth
Type of planet	Rocky	Rocky	Rocky
Atmosphere	None	CO_2, N_2	N_2, O_2
Mean distance from the Sun (Earth = 1)	0.3871	0.7233	1
Sidereal period of orbit (years)	0.24	0.62	1
Equatorial radius (km)	2,439	6,052	6,378
Equatorial radius (miles)	1,515.5	3,760.5	3,963.1
Length of day (hours)	1,408	5,832	23.93
Number of observed satellites	0	0	1

AIR FRICTION

When spacecraft enters the atmosphere of a planet, friction with the molecules of air causes the spacecraft to heat up. A similar thing happens when you rub the palms of your hands together briskly. You will feel them warming up. This warming is caused by friction. If two objects rub against one another fast enough, a great deal of heat can be created. Campers can start a fire by rapidly rubbing two pieces of wood together. An automobile needs oil to keep its moving parts from being damaged by friction.

Air may not seem like something that would be likely to cause much friction. No matter how hard you wave your hand around, you will hardly feel anything at all. But air can cause a great deal of friction if something is moving fast enough. Meteors streaking through the night sky are tiny pieces of rock or metal heated to a brilliant white glow from friction with the air. Most meteors burn up completely.

A returning spacecraft has to deal with the same friction. To keep them from burning up, spacecraft are equipped with heat shields. Heat shields are protective barriers that prevent the heat caused by friction from burning up the spacecraft.

Mars	Jupiter	Saturn	Uranus	Neptune	Pluto
Rocky	Gas giant	Gas giant	Gas giant	Gas giant	Ice dwarf
CO_2, N_2, Ar	H_2, He	H_2, He	H_2, He, CH_4	H_2, He CH_4	None
1.524	5.203	9.539	19.19	30.06	39.48
1.88	11.86	29.46	84.01	164.79	247.92
3,397	71,492	60,268	25,559	24,764	1,151
2,110.8	44,423	37,448.8	15,881.6	15,388	715
24.62	9.92	10.66	17.24	16.11	153.3
2	62	59	27	13	3

During each orbit, *Magellan*'s radar mapper imaged a swath of the planet's surface approximately 10 to 17 miles (17 to 28 km) wide. At the end of each orbit, the spacecraft radioed back to Earth the image of a long ribbon-like strip of the planet's surface.

By the end of its first 243-day cycle, *Magellan* had sent to Earth detailed images of 84 percent of Venus's surface. *Magellan* did this twice more between 1991 and 1992, eventually creating detailed maps of 98 percent of Venus. Having duplicate maps allowed scientists to detect any changes that might have occurred on the surface between cycles. *Magellan* also took images from slightly different

Magellan's radar created images of almost the entire surface of Venus in great detail. Radar does not take actual photos but, instead, detects differences in surface texture. Smooth areas appear dark, while rough areas appear bright. Scientists take this information and create three-dimensional images, such as this one. The color is added by computer to make the image look more realistic.

angles, enabling scientists to reconstruct realistic three-dimensional views of the planet's surface.

Ultimately, *Magellan* created the first near-photographic quality, ultrahigh resolution mapping of the planet's surface features. It revealed features as small as 300 feet (91 m). Prior Venus missions had created low-resolution radar globes of general, continent-sized formations. *Magellan*, however, finally allowed detailed imaging and analysis of craters, hills, ridges, and other geologic formations. These images are similar to the visible-light photographic mapping of other planets. *Magellan*'s global radar map will remain the most detailed Venus map in existence for the foreseeable future. No space agency currently has plans for any robotic mission to try to surpass its resolution.

At the end of *Magellan*'s mission, several experiments were devoted to investigating Venus's gravitational pull. The spacecraft swung so low in its orbit that it grazed the upper reaches of Venus's atmosphere. This grazing caused *Magellan*'s orbit to degrade even further. Eventually, as planned, *Magellan* plunged into the planet's atmosphere in 1994 and was vaporized, although some pieces might have hit the planet's surface.

4

Of all the planets in our solar system, Mars has received the most intense interest from scientists, going back hundreds of years. While layers of dense clouds hide the surfaces of Venus, Jupiter, and Saturn, Mars is an entirely different matter.

Although Mars is a small world and far from Earth, even the earliest astronomers could see through their telescopes that the planet was not hiding behind a veil of clouds. They observed the actual surface features of another world, although the surface features weren't very clear. While astronomers could just make out a bright polar cap and dusky markings, they didn't know what those markings actually were. Before the beginning of the twentieth century, many astronomers thought the dark areas might be seas and the orange regions separating them might be vast deserts.

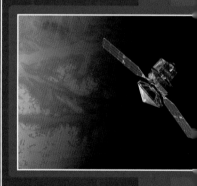

Two men—neither of them professional scientists—made Mars even more fascinating to scientists as well as the general public. In 1877 an Italian astronomer named Giovanni Schiaparelli thought he saw faint

Top: One of the first views of the Martian surface taken by the *Viking 1* lander. *Center:* The *Sojourner* rover was the first wheeled vehicle to explore Mars. *Bottom:* The *Mars Reconnaissance Orbiter* has sent valuable data to Earth regarding the presence of water on Mars.

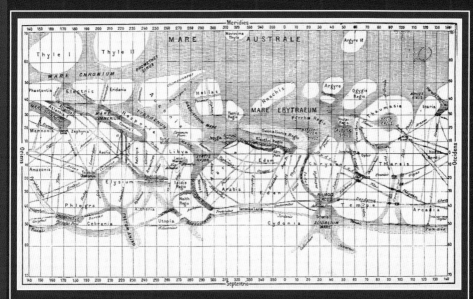

Giovanni Schiaparelli's 1877 map of Mars started the controversy about the existence of canals on the planet.

linear markings on the Martian surface. He called these *canali*, the Italian word for channel, a natural feature. But the word also looks a lot like the English word *canal*, which is not a natural feature by any means.

A wealthy Bostonian and avid amateur astronomer named Percival Lowell took the word *canal* literally. He believed that the lines Schiaparelli saw were real canals, or artificial channels created by intelligent creatures. He believed this so fervently that he financed the construction of a major observatory in Flagstaff, Arizona, for the sole purpose of studying the red planet (Mars). (The Lowell Observatory is still there and very active in astronomical research—especially the study of Mars.)

Lowell also lectured widely and wrote two very popular books: *Mars* (1895) and *Mars as the Abode of Life* (1910). He described a dying race of Martians, far more advanced technologically than the people on Earth. He said that the Martians were desperately trying to survive the drying up of their planet by pumping vast quantities of water from the polar caps through a complex system of canals. This description caught the imaginations of thousands of people. Many other astronomers started focusing their attention on Mars. Many of them saw canals as clearly as Lowell did, but most of these astronomers were either amateurs or professionals using very small instruments. Astronomers using the largest, best telescopes in the world saw nothing but vague, random markings and no canals.

Inspired by Lowell's image of Mars, science-fiction writers poured out dozens of stories and novels, most of which involved travelers from Earth landing on the red planet and discovering some sort of ideal civilization of human beings. H. G. Wells changed that forever. His novel, *The War of the Worlds*, was the first to describe hostile aliens from Mars in a full-scale alien invasion of Earth. The story was also one of the first science-fiction stories to consider the possibility that aliens from another planet might not look anything at all like humans. Not only was this book an instant best seller, it made Mars a permanent fixture in people's imaginations. Space travel and Mars became almost synonymous.

By the 1950s, improved instruments and observations had revealed that Mars is a cold, dry world with only a very thin atmosphere. But tantalizing questions still remained, especially: is there life on Mars? When humans first started sending probes to other worlds, Mars was at the top of the list.

THE RED PLANET

The Soviet Union launched the first Mars probes from Earth. They launched the two *Marsnik* spacecraft in October 1960, but both failed to reach orbit around Earth. Other Soviet probes to Mars had no better luck.

LOOKING FOR LIFE

While countless different scientific experiments and investigations have been performed in space, two questions have fascinated scientists more than any others. The first is how the solar system and planet Earth came to be. The other is whether life exists anywhere else in the solar system. Or if life on another planet in the solar system doesn't exist now, could it have existed in the past? Or do conditions exist somewhere that might cause life to develop at some time in the future?

For more than a century, planetary astronomers have made Mars a major focus of attention. More robotic probes have been sent to that planet than to any other. The search for life has largely driven this interest. Until the 1970s, no planets in the solar system other than Earth and Mars seemed likely to have ever sparked life.

As modern scientists learn more about the conditions under which life can evolve and thrive, the search for life in the solar system has grown beyond Mars. Scientists have found that life can exist under conditions harsher than anyone had ever thought possible. So scientists have been expanding their area of research. Life might need only access to the right chemicals and elements and a source of energy in order to evolve. Life may have evolved, for instance, in the vast ocean that exists beneath the icy crust of Europa (one of Jupiter's moons) or in the chemical-rich clouds of Jupiter.

The first successful mission to Mars finally occurred in 1964. The U.S. spacecraft *Mariner 4* took twenty-one photos as it flew past the planet. The results were not very encouraging. The probe revealed that Mars had only 1 percent of Earth's atmosphere and consisted almost entirely of carbon dioxide. The photos were even more discouraging. They revealed that Mars was as cratered and desolate looking as the Moon. Many disappointed scientists wanted to discontinue their research, but the little red planet still had some surprises to reveal.

Five years later, *Mariner 6* and *7* flew past Mars. Again, the planet looked desolate and uninviting—not a good place to look for life. *Mariner 9*, however, launched in 1971, changed scientists' minds. Instead of a flyby, during which a probe could take only a handful of photos of a small area of the planet, *Mariner 9* went into orbit. It was the first spacecraft ever to orbit another planet. *Mariner 9* had plenty of time to take pictures and gather data, so scientists hoped that it would finally resolve some of their unanswered questions.

But the first photos *Mariner 9* sent back were almost completely blank! An enormous dust storm hid the surface of Mars

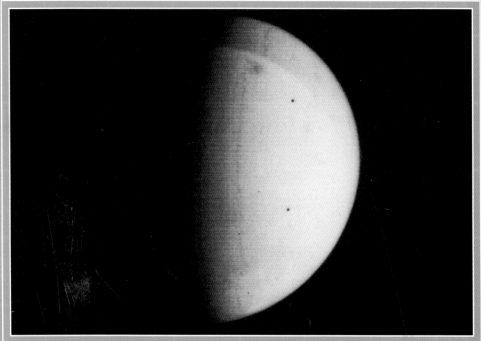

One of *Mariner 9*'s first images of Mars showed a disappointing blank planet. The spacecraft had arrived at the same time as a planetwide dust storm. Fortunately, the dust settled before it was too late, and *Mariner 9* obtained many great photos. Although scientists didn't realize it at the time, the small, round, gray smudge near the upper edge of the planet is the summit of Olympus Mons—the largest, tallest volcano in the solar system. (The two small black specks were created by the camera. They are part of a grid that allows scientists to correct any distortion in the photo.)

beneath clouds that covered it from pole to pole. Scientists could see only three small dusky spots in the otherwise featureless clouds. They had to sit back and wait patiently for the storm to end. It took nearly a month, but the wait was worth it.

As the dust finally began to settle, astronomers were astonished to discover that the dusky spots were in fact the summits of enormous volcanoes. The mountains were so high that their cratered peaks penetrated through the top of the dust storm. As the dust storm cleared, the photos showed four huge mountains higher than any on Earth. Other features also began to appear. Bright circular patches marked the locations of craters. A bright, meandering streak turned out to be a dust-filled canyon 155 miles (250 km) wide, up to 4 miles (7 km) deep, and 2,300 miles (3700 km) long. It wrapped a fifth of the way around Mars and was larger than any canyon on Earth. Even more amazing, some features appeared to have been caused by the erosion of water.

The Soviet Union also sent more probes to Mars. *Mars 3* managed to land on the planet in 1971, but it fell silent after only twenty seconds. After a number of unsuccessful probes, the Soviets gave up altogether. The Soviet vehicles however, were the first human artifacts to touch the surface of Mars.

VIKING 1 AND VIKING 2

In August and September 1975, NASA launched a pair of probes to Mars—*Viking 1* and *Viking 2*. Scientists had decided to send two probes to study two different areas on Mars. Also, one could act as a backup in case the other failed.

The probes arrived nearly three weeks apart in July and August 1976. Both spacecraft consisted of two parts, an orbiter and a lander. For sixteen days, *Viking 1* circled the planet, surveying its surface for

The *Viking 2* lander took this self-portrait on September 3, 1976. It is one of the first photos ever taken on the surface of Mars. The pink sky was a complete surprise to scientists, who had at first thought it was a mistake on the part of the lander's camera.

potential landing sites. NASA scientists chose a landing spot in a plain called Chryse Planitia and released the lander. It descended slowly at first by parachutes and then, as it neared the surface, by rockets. It touched down on July 20. Several weeks later, *Viking 2* landed in a spot called Utopia Planitia.

Panoramic photos revealed reddish deserts strewn with dark rocks. But the color of the sky surprised scientists the most. Instead of the dark blue everyone had expected, it was pink! The high concentration of dust in the atmosphere created this color. The atmosphere itself consisted almost totally of carbon dioxide, with 2.7 percent nitrogen and traces of argon, oxygen, and water vapor.

The probes found no sign of life on Mars. The lander's miniature laboratory didn't detect any carbon-based atoms and compounds in the soil that are necessary for life to exist. Other experiments to look for signs of living organisms returned unclear results. A few scientists claimed the experiments revealed signs of life, while most others said they were merely the result of ordinary chemical reactions. Scientists continue to debate the results of the Viking experiments.

As the landers analyzed the Martian soil and took measurements on the surface, the two orbiters mapped the surface. They took more than forty thousand photos in all. Many photos captured features as small as 33 feet (10 m). With this data, scientists created the first detailed map of Mars. The orbiters and landers continued to transmit data for several more years. The *Viking 1* orbiter made its last transmission in November 1982.

AFTER VIKING

The European Space Agency (ESA)—a group of seventeen nations that have pooled their resources for space exploration—launched its first Mars mission, Mars Express, in June 1993. Like the Viking mission, Mars Express consisted of an orbiter and a lander called the *Beagle-2*. Unfortunately, the ESA lost all contact with the *Beagle-2* soon after its release from the orbiter.

The *Mars Express* orbiter worked perfectly and has returned valuable information. This includes strong evidence of the presence of water ice on Mars and erosion features created by water flowing on the surface of ancient Mars. *Mars Express* has taken some of the most spectacular photos of the planet. Its High Resolution Stereo Color Camera (HRSC) produces detailed, three-dimensional images of features as small as 6.5 feet (2 m).

An artist's impression shows ESA's *Mars Express* orbiter over Mars.

NASA launched the *Mars Global Surveyor (MGS)* on November 7, 1996. This was the first successful U.S. mission to the red planet in twenty years. The spacecraft reached the target orbit around Mars on September 12, 1997. The spacecraft began its primary mission of mapping Mars in March 1999. Its low-altitude polar orbit—at 240 miles (380 km)—allowed it to observe every region of the Martian surface as the planet rotated beneath it. Its telescopic cameras snapped images revealing details as small as 3 feet (1 m). *MGS* has returned more data about the red planet than all other Mars missions combined. The spacecraft gathered data about the Martian surface as well as its atmosphere and interior, including data on the composition of the surface, ice, atmospheric dust, and clouds.

Perhaps most important, the Mars Orbiter Laser Altimeter (MOLA) accurately measured the height of surface features. The MOLA bounced hundreds of millions of laser pulses off the Martian surface and measured the time it took for the light to make the round-trip. The shorter the time it took for a pulse to return, the closer the surface was to the spacecraft. This indicated higher terrain. The longer it took for the pulse to return, the lower the surface. With these measurements, scientists created an accurate topographic map of Mars—that is, a map that shows the three-dimensional contours of the planet. For the first time, scientists knew the exact height of the tallest mountain in the solar system, Olympus Mons: 84,500 feet (25,800 m). In comparison, Earth's Mount Everest is only 29,035 feet (8,850 m) high.

MGS also provided clear evidence that Mars once had a large supply of liquid water. *MGS* showed that a great deal of this water may still remain on the planet in the form of huge reservoirs of

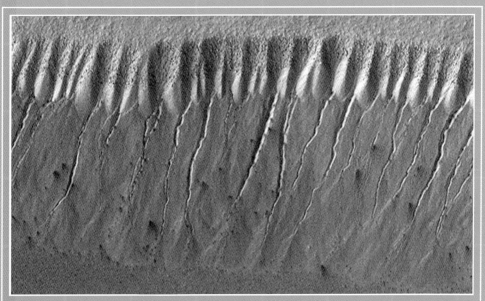

One of the most significant discoveries made by the *Mars Global Surveyor* is clear signs of the presence of water on Mars. This image of gullies on the side of a valley may have been created very recently by water flowing from the face of the cliff.

underground ice. Evidence for flowing water includes many different types of erosion features, such as channels, riverbeds, and gullies.

WHEELS ON MARS

NASA launched *Mars Pathfinder* in December 1996 as part of its policy of achieving smaller, less expensive planetary missions. NASA sent smaller probes into space using smaller, less expensive launch vehicles. The probes were cheaper to build because NASA used existing materials instead of custommade instruments and equipment.

NASA also used a new method for landing *Pathfinder* on Mars. Like the Viking landers, a parachute slowed *Pathfinder*'s descent through the thin Martian atmosphere. But instead of making a soft landing using rockets, a cluster of balloonlike air bags—each one 17 feet (5 m) in diameter—inflated around the lander. As soon as they fully inflated, the cluster cut loose from the parachute. The cluster of air bags fell to the surface, bouncing and rolling like a huge beach ball until finally coming to rest. Then the air bags deflated to reveal the lander, which opened its three solar panels as well as the ramps that allowed the rover *Sojourner* to roll down onto the Martian surface. (NASA named the rover after U.S. abolitionist and women's rights campaigner Sojourner Truth.)

Touchdown occurred on July 4, 1997. The landing site, an ancient floodplain in Mars's northern hemisphere, known as Ares Vallis, is one of the rockiest parts of Mars. Because the plain didn't have many large craters, mountains, or canyons, scientists believed it was a relatively safe surface to land on. The spot also has a wide variety of rocks that were deposited during what appeared to be a catastrophic flood millions of years earlier. Following its successful touchdown, the lander was formally named the Carl Sagan Memorial

Station, after the late Cornell University astronomer who widely pop-ularized astronomy in the 1970s and 1980s.

Sojourner was a tiny, boxlike vehicle resembling a toaster on six wheels. It weighed only 24 pounds (11 kg). However, scientists packed it with instruments, including lasers, temperature sensors, cameras, communications equipment, and special tools for studying rocks and soil. *Sojourner* trundled along at a top speed of 2 feet (0.6 m) a minute. It moved from rock to rock, taking close-up photos and analyzing their chemical and physical makeup.

The Mars Pathfinder mission returned 2.6 gigabytes—which is equivalent to about 347,000 CDs—of information about Martian soil,

After *Pathfinder* set down on Mars, it released the tiny *Sojourner* rover *(below)*, which stood only 11 inches (28 cm) high and weighed just 24 pounds (11 kg). Except for its wheels, most of *Sojourner* is hidden under its solar power panel. Here it is seen trundling toward a rock, one of the first it will examine with its special instruments.

One of the first views of the Martian surface *(above)* taken by *Pathfinder* reveals a plain of red dust and black volcanic rocks under a pink sky.

Sojourner took this close-up photo *(above)* of a Martian rock. Its pitted surface suggests that it is a chunk of ancient lava.

rocks, and atmosphere, including more than 16,500 images from the lander and 550 images from the rover. It also returned more than fifteen chemical analyses of rocks and soil and extensive data on winds

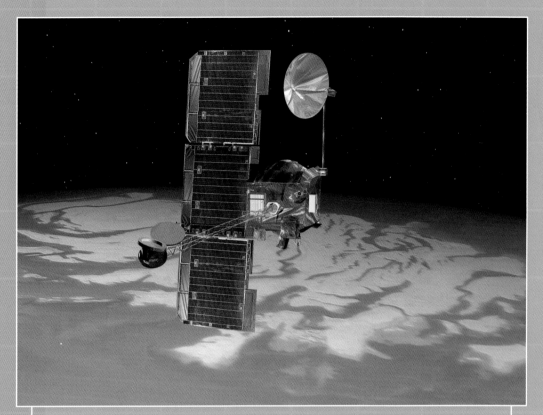

Mars Odyssey, seen here in an artist's impression, passes over the south pole on Mars. It has been mapping Mars and searching for water on the planet since 2001.

and other weather phenomena. Most important, scientists learned that at some time in its past, Mars had a much thicker atmosphere and liquid water. The *Pathfinder* confirmed this suspicion when it discovered minerals that could have formed only in water. Three months after touchdown, the rover's rechargeable batteries finally died due to the cold temperatures. The entire mission was considered an enormous success since NASA only expected it to last one month.

ROVING OVER MARS

NASA launched two more rovers to Mars in 2003. The first of the Mars Exploration Rovers, *Spirit*, landed on the planet on January 4, 2004. The second rover, *Opportunity*, landed on January 25. So far, the

MARS EXPLORATION ROVERS

The two rovers that landed on Mars in 2004 were far more sophisticated machines than little *Sojourner*. Each rover is 5.2 feet (1.6 m) long, weighs 384 pounds (174 kg), and can travel up to 120 inches (300 cm) a minute. Powered by large solar panels that look like huge insect wings, the rovers carry lots of equipment.

They hold spectrometers that can determine the elements in a substance by analyzing the light it emits or reflects. The rovers have dust collectors, robotic arms, and automated laboratories for analyzing samples. Special cameras allowed scientists to obtain the first-ever microscopic images of Martian rocks and soil.

This is an artistic rendering of one of the two identical Mars Exploration Rovers. The flat wings are solar panels for generating power. The tall, white mast supports a pair of cameras, while the jointed arm in front carries surface sampling tools. Each wheel is independently powered and suspended, allowing the vehicle to cross over any terrain.

rovers have covered thousands of yards from their landing sites in a mission that was supposed to have lasted only ninety days.

On March 23, 2004, NASA held a news conference and announced a major discovery in the search for evidence of past liquid water on the Martian surface. Scientists displayed pictures and data revealing layers within the rocks inside a crater at *Opportunity*'s landing site, Meridiani Planum. These layers showed stratification and "cross-bedding," which are features that occur on Earth when flowing water lays down sediment, or layers of

This image shows some of the thousands of "blueberries" found by the *Opportunity* rover. These small, pea-sized rocks are strong evidence that water once flowed on Mars. They are made of a mineral called hematite, which can only form in the presence of water.

silt. The rover also discovered jarosite, a mineral that uses water to form. Additionally, scientists found irregular distribution of the elements chlorine and bromine. This finding suggested that the location had been the shoreline of a salty sea that had long ago evaporated.

Finally, scientists saw what looked like strange rocks they called "blueberries" scattered all over one area, like thousands of spilled BB pellets. These small, dark, perfectly round objects are thought to be made of hematite, an iron-bearing mineral that only forms in the presence of water. Scientists believe the hematite pellets may have been deposited by salty water millions of years ago.

On April 30, 2004, after driving 656 feet (200 m) in five days, *Opportunity* arrived at a crater named Endurance. After it left Endurance crater, it visited Victoria crater. Since craters are essentially

An artist's depiction of *Opportunity* rover on the rim of Victoria crater

holes punched in the crust of Mars, they allow scientists to look deeply beneath the surface.

On February 7, 2006, *Spirit* reached the semicircular rock formation known as Home Plate. It is a layered rock outcrop that puzzles, yet fascinates, scientists. They think that Home Plate's rocks are explosive volcanic deposits. Other possibilities exist, however, including impact deposits or perhaps sediment deposited by wind or water. *Spirit* later explored the Columbia hills, which at first seemed impossibly out of reach. The hills are many miles farther than the rover was meant to travel.

Spirit and *Opportunity* have lasted more than seven times longer than NASA expected. In March 2006, the age of the rovers finally began to catch up with them. *Spirit*'s front right wheel stopped working. Its operators took much of the strain off the injured wheel by turning *Spirit* around and driving it backward, letting the broken wheel drag behind. Two asteroids, 37452 Spirit and 39382 Opportunity, have been named in honor of the rovers and the great deal of data they have gathered.

MARS RECONNAISSANCE ORBITER

NASA's *Mars Reconnaissance Orbiter* (*MRO*) is the most recent robotic mission to Mars. Launched in August 2005, it arrived in orbit around Mars in March 2006. Similar in many ways to the *Mars Surveyor Orbiter*, *MRO* carries the most powerful telescopic camera ever to scrutinize the surface of the red planet. It can capture sharp pictures of objects on the surface as small as 1 foot (0.3 m) from an altitude of 186 miles (300 km).

MRO also contains the Mars Color Imager (MARCI), a wide-angle, low-resolution camera that looks at the surface of Mars in visible and ultraviolet light. Each day MARCI collects about eighty-four images. Being able to compare changes on Mars from day to day instead of month to month enables scientists to accurately determine Mars's seasonal variations and to better understand how the weather on Mars works. They are then able to measure the changing amounts of water vapor in the Martian atmosphere and to track its movements as the seasons change.

MRO's mission is planned to last for two Earth years. One of the goals is to map the Martian landscape with high-resolution cameras to choose landing sites for future missions. In addition, radar will penetrate the ice at the polar caps to see what kind of terrain lies beneath. A spectrometer will measure temperature, pressure, water vapor, and dust levels.

An artist's impression shows the *Mars Reconnaissance Orbiter* high above Mars. In the first six months of operation, it sent enough information back to Earth to fill two thousand CDs.

5

Before the age of space exploration, everything scientists knew about Jupiter came from what they could see through Earth-based telescopes. They knew that Jupiter is the largest planet. In fact, it is larger than all the other planets combined. They knew that it is composed mainly of hydrogen and helium. It also has small amounts of methane, ammonia, water vapor, traces of other compounds, and possibly a core of rock and ice. They could see the colorful cloud bands and storms that indicated a dynamic weather system. They also knew that the planet completes one orbit of the Sun each 11.8 Earth years and that its day is nine hours fifty-five minutes long.

As long ago as 1610, Galileo had observed that Jupiter has four very large moons, one of which is nearly the size of the planet Mercury. (Scientists later determined that the giant planet has more than six moons.) But what lay beneath those colorful clouds? Was there a solid surface? Or did Jupiter's atmosphere blend into its core? Where did Jupiter get the

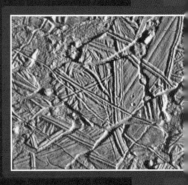

Top: An artist's impression of one of the *Voyager* spacecraft. *Center:* One of the thousands of detailed photos of Jupiter sent to Earth by the *Galileo* orbiter. *Bottom: Galileo* took this close-up photo of the giant ice floes that cover the surface of Jupiter's large moon, Europa.

energy to drive its powerful storms? These and hundreds of other questions could only be answered by sending robot explorers.

THE PIONEERS

Human exploration of the outer solar system began with NASA's launch of *Pioneer 10* on March 2, 1972. At that time, *Pioneer 10* was the fastest human-made object to leave Earth. It was fast enough to pass the Moon in eleven hours and to cross the orbit of Mars, about 50 million miles (80 million km) away, in just twelve weeks.

    Pioneer 10 would be going 600 million miles (1 billion km) away, so sunlight would not work for generating power. So instead of using solar panels for power, NASA equipped the spacecraft with a nuclear thermoelectric power generator. This device carried plutonium, a radioactive element. The heat from the plutonium's radioactive decay

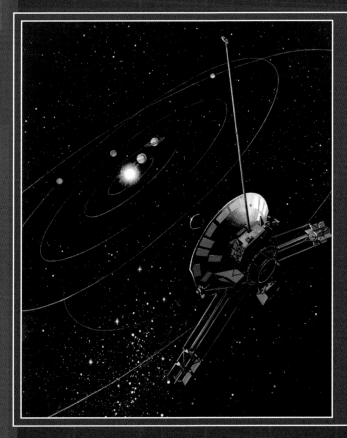

An artist's impression shows one of the *Pioneer* spacecraft. The large, dish-shaped antenna enabled the spacecraft to communicate with Earth. The two booms sticking out at the bottom and the right on the spacecraft held the nuclear power sources that generate electricity. And the long boom at the top carried a magneto-meter for measuring magnetic fields.

Pioneer 10 took this image of Jupiter as it flew past the planet in 1972. Although it doesn't reveal much detail, it is still a better view of the planet than Earth-based astronomers had ever been able to see.

was converted to electricity. Communicating with Earth would also be a problem from such a distance. A large 9-foot (2.7 m) diameter dish antenna was continually pointed at Earth by spinning the spacecraft around the central axis of the antenna at a leisurely five revolutions per minute—the speed of a barbecue rotisserie.

After 180 days, the spacecraft became the first human-made object to cross the asteroid belt and measure how much dust it contained. The asteroid belt is a region between Mars and Jupiter occupied by thousands of rocky and metallic bodies, ranging in size from only a few feet to many miles. Two months later, *Pioneer 10* reached Jupiter. The long trip took twenty-one months to complete.

Pioneer 10 accelerated by the massive planet to a speed of 82,000 miles per hour (132,000 km/hr) and passed within 81,000 miles (130,354 km) of Jupiter's cloud tops on December 3, 1973. During the flyby, the spacecraft took three hundred photos, the first-ever close-up images of the planet. It also charted Jupiter's lethally powerful radiation belts, which proved to be ten thousand times more powerful than the Van Allen belts that surround Earth. *Pioneer*'s electronics survived the scathing radiation, which would be deadly to humans.

THE GRAVITATIONAL SLINGSHOT

The motion of a planet can be used to alter the path and speed of an interplanetary spacecraft. This maneuver is often used on missions to the outer planets, which would otherwise be prohibitively expensive, if not impossible, to reach with current technologies. The maneuver is known as a gravitational slingshot.

So where is the slingshot? Remember that the planets are not standing still. They are moving in their orbits around the Sun.

If the planet is moving relative to the Sun, the approaching spacecraft can gain momentum. Depending on the direction of the outbound leg of the trajectory, the spacecraft can gain up to twice the orbital speed of the planet. In the case of Jupiter, this is more than 29,000 miles per hour (46,800 km/h). You can see a similar phenomenon for yourself by rolling a steel ball past a moving magnet. The magnet will pull the ball along, adding to its original speed.

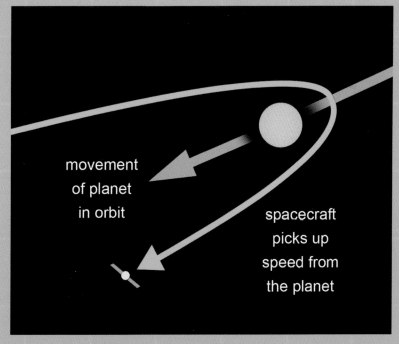

movement
of planet
in orbit

spacecraft
picks up
speed from
the planet

In a gravitational slingshot, a spacecraft uses the orbital speed of a planet to increase its own speed and to change the direction of its flight at the same time. The effect is similar to bouncing a plastic ball off the front of a moving car. The ball changes direction and picks up speed from the car.

NASA launched *Pioneer 11* one year later in April 1973. After a safe passage through the asteroid belt, it passed by Jupiter on December 2, 1974—26,725 miles (43,000 km) above its cloud tops. *Pioneer 11* took dramatic images of the Great Red Spot, a vast storm the size of Earth. It also made the first observation of the immense polar regions and determined the mass of Callisto, one of Jupiter's large moons.

Pioneer 10 and *11* were both accelerated by Jupiter's gravitational slingshot. *Pioneer 10* was literally thrown out of the solar system, the first human-made object to travel outside the solar system. In about 8 million years, it will reach the star Aldebaran. *Pioneer 11* approached Jupiter close enough to be accelerated to a velocity of 108,000 miles per hour (173,000 km/h)—fifty-five times that of a high-speed rifle bullet. This velocity gave the spacecraft enough of a boost to send it 1.5 billion miles (2.4 billion km) to Saturn. The two Pioneers returned valuable information about Jupiter. They also paved the way for later, more sophisticated spacecraft. In this sense, they really were true pioneers.

THE VOYAGERS

NASA scientists had been using the gravity of planets to boost the speed and change the direction of spacecraft. They began to realize that the outer planets—Jupiter, Saturn, Uranus, and Neptune—were lining up in a useful way. A single spacecraft could visit all four large outer planets one after the other with minimum fuel using the gravitational slingshot effect. The spacecraft would be slung from one planet to another like a pinball in an arcade game. This ambitious expedition was originally called the Grand Tour.

NASA scientists developed two spacecraft to take advantage of the coming alignment. *Voyager 1* was launched in September 1977,

A GREETING CARD TO THE UNIVERSE

Scientists knew that the Pioneer spacecraft would be going fast enough to eventually leave the solar system altogether. So they attached a message from Earth to each spacecraft. They attached a gold-plated aluminum plaque engraved with a drawing of a human male and female, along with a diagram of Earth's location in the Milky Way. The British aero- space engineer Eric Burgess origi- nally suggested the idea to U.S. astronomer Carl Sagan. Sagan and fellow astronomer Frank Drake designed the plaque. Sagan's wife, Linda Salzman Sagan, pre- pared the artwork. The plaque also contains diagrams of the space- craft and of the solar system. It even identifies the Sun's position in our galactic neighborhood.

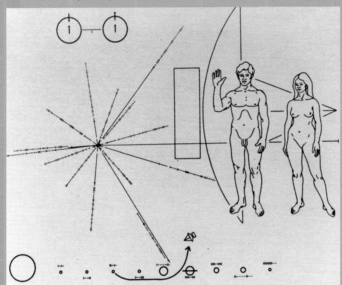

Knowing that *Pioneer 10* would be the first human-made object to ever leave the solar system, engineers attached this plaque to it. It shows the location of Earth within the galaxy as well as pictures of two human beings standing in front of the spacecraft.

shortly after its sister craft, *Voyager 2*. Although NASA launched *Voyager 1* after *Voyager 2*, it was on a faster trajectory, so it reached Jupiter and Saturn first.

    Voyager 1 began photographing Jupiter in January 1979. Its clos- est approach to Jupiter was on March 5, 1979, when it was 217,000 miles (349,000 km) from the center of the planet. *Voyager 2* made its closest approach to Jupiter on July 9, 1979, coming within 350,000 miles (563,000 km) of the planet's cloud tops. The Voyager cameras were of much higher resolution than those in the Pioneer spacecraft, allowing scientists to study the planet and many of its moons in greater detail. Imaging started eighty days before *Voyager 1*'s closest encounter with Jupiter. By ten days before its closest approach, *Voyager 1* was returning pictures better than any Pioneer has sent.

In addition to studying the giant planet itself, the spacecraft also trained their instruments on Jupiter's four largest moons, revealing each to be distinctly—and often surprisingly—different from the others. Callisto revealed a huge impact feature that had left concentric rings 620 miles (1,000 km) wide on its icy surface, like the frozen ripples in a pond. Europa was as smooth as a cue ball, with thousands of linear features stretching for hundreds of miles across its surface. Ganymede showed strange brown and white patches. Io showed one of the most surprising discoveries—the existence of active volcanoes. Io eventually proved to be the most volcanically active body in the solar system. Plumes from its supervolcanoes extend more than 190 miles (300 km) into space.

As *Voyager 1* was leaving the Jupiter system, it took a time exposure image of the planet backlit by the Sun. When scientists

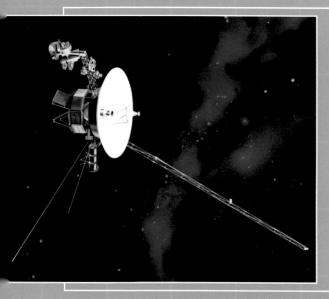

An artist's depiction shows one of the Voyager spacecraft floating in space. The upper arm carried cameras and other instruments. The small blue cylinder on the lower part is the spacecraft's nuclear power source. The long arm carries a magnetometer for measuring the magnetic fields of planets.

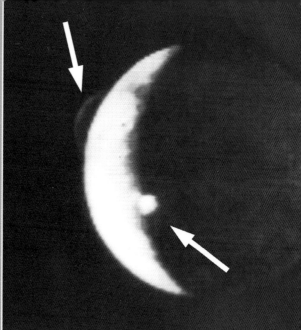

In 1979 *Voyager 1* returned the best images of Jupiter *(left)* ever obtained up until that time. Near the center of the planet is the Great Red Spot, a vast hurricanelike storm that covers an area as large as Earth. This *Voyager 2* photo *(right)* was the first ever taken of the volcanoes on Io— two of which are indicated by arrows. Scientists later found out that Io is the most volcanically active body in the solar system.

examined the photo, they were surprised to see a faint, dusty ring of material circling Jupiter. Unlike Saturn's rings, which are brilliantly white because they are made of almost pure ice, Jupiter's rings are made of very fine dark dust. In addition to the ring, scientists found two new, small satellites, Adrastea and Metis, orbiting just outside the planet. Scientists discovered a third new satellite, Thebe, orbiting between Amalthea, one of Jupiter's innermost moons, and Io.

GALILEO

The launch of the *Galileo* probe did not go as planned. According to the original plan, the *Challenger* space shuttle would have carried the probe and its Centaur rocket booster into orbit. But tragically, the *Challenger* exploded during takeoff in 1986. Scientists had to wait until NASA made safety changes to its shuttle fleet before they could launch *Galileo*.

Galileo had to perform several gravitational slingshots (once by Venus and twice by Earth) to reach the velocity required to get to its destination—Jupiter. Along the way, *Galileo* closely observed the asteroids 951 Gaspra and 243 Ida and discovered Ida's tiny moon, Dactyl. The smallest moon yet discovered, Dactyl is only about 1 mile (1.6 km) wide. It has so little gravity that an astronaut on its surface could throw a baseball that would never come down.

Galileo's prime mission was a two-year study of the Jupiter system. Unlike the previous Pioneer and Voyager missions, the *Galileo*

An artist's impression shows *Galileo* circling Jupiter. The golden petallike structure on the left is the antenna meant to send signals back to Earth. It should have opened like an umbrella but failed to do so. For this reason, *Galileo* couldn't send nearly as many images as scientists had hoped. Still, *Galileo* sent fourteen thousand pictures back to Earth.

Galileo took this portrait of Jupiter in 1995. In the extraordinary images *Galileo* sent back to Earth, scientists could see the planet in more detail than ever before.

spacecraft would orbit Jupiter, with each orbit lasting about two months. The orbits were designed to allow the spacecraft to make close-up flybys of several of Jupiter's largest moons. Altogether, *Galileo* orbited Jupiter thirty-five times.

In addition to taking thousands of highly detailed photos, *Galileo* performed many scientific experiments. It discovered ammonia in the atmosphere of Jupiter. It was the first time this important organic mole-cule had been observed in the atmosphere of another planet. The spacecraft closely observed the volcanic activity on Io that *Pioneer 11* had discovered, revealing that it is a hundred times greater than the activity on Earth. *Galileo* also discovered that a powerful electrical current connects Io with Jupiter.

In 1994 *Galileo* was perfectly positioned to watch the fragments of comet Shoemaker-Levy 9 crash into Jupiter. Terrestrial telescopes had to wait to see the enormous impact sites as they rotated into view. This was one of the most important astronomical events of the twentieth century.

Scientists had long known that asteroids and comets had collided with the planets in the past. The thousands of giant craters on the Moon, Mars, and other worlds are evidence of past collisions. Even Earth has scars of ancient impacts, although erosion has erased most of them. But scientists were surprised and excited that such large-scale impacts were still going on. They also realized that Earth itself was not immune to impacts.

Scientists created this image of Jupiter's volcanic moon Io from the best photos taken by *Galileo*. The large and small dark spots are volcanic areas, surrounded by colorful sulfur deposits. Io has more active volcanoes erupting at any one time than Earth does.

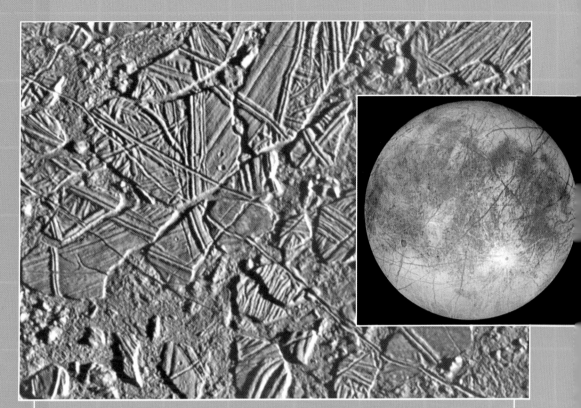

Galileo took this image *(inset)* of Europa, one of Jupiter's four largest moons. The lines that crisscross its surface are actually huge cracks in an icy crust floating on top of a vast ocean of liquid water. *Galileo* also took this close-up image of Europa's surface *(above)*, which shows its jumbled ice floes. This jigsaw is created when the surface ice breaks up and refreezes. It closely resembles ice floes in Earth's Arctic and Antarctic areas.

Perhaps *Galileo*'s most exciting discovery was the evidence for a vast ocean of liquid water under the icy crust of Europa. Many scientists believe that this may be one of the best places to look for life in the solar system.

On September 21, 2003, after fourteen years in space and eight years in orbit around Jupiter, *Galileo* was allowed to plunge into Jupiter's atmosphere, where it vaporized. Scientists feared that if they left *Galileo* in orbit, it might one day crash into a moon. This crash could contaminate the moon with organisms from Earth that may have inadvertently survived aboard the spacecraft.

Cassini at Jupiter

Cassini-Huygens was a joint mission of the European Space Agency and NASA. While on its way to Saturn, *Cassini* made a close approach to Jupiter on December 30, 2000, and performed many scientific measurements. It took about twenty-six thousand images of Jupiter during the course of the months long flyby. *Cassini* produced the most detailed global color portrait of Jupiter. The smallest visible features are approximately 40 miles (60 km) across.

The *Cassini-Huygens* probe was one of the largest ever to be sent into space.

The Jupiter flyby made a major discovery about the nature of Jupiter's atmospheric circulation. Dark belts alternate with light zones in the atmosphere. Scientists had long considered the zones, with their pale clouds, to be areas of upwelling air, partly because many clouds on Earth form where air is rising. Analysis of *Cassini* imagery, however, told a new story. Individual storm cells of upwelling bright-white clouds, too small to see from Earth, pop up almost without exception in the dark belts.

Other observations of the atmosphere included a swirling dark oval of high-atmosphere haze, about the size of the Great Red Spot, near Jupiter's north pole. Infrared imagery revealed aspects of circulation near the poles, with bands of globe-encircling winds and

Io seems to float among the clouds of distant Jupiter in this image taken by the *Cassini* probe as it passed by the giant planet.

adjacent bands moving in opposite directions. All of these data gave scientists clues as to what might be going on deep within the giant planet. Unlike the weather of Earth, which receives all of its energy from the Sun, Jupiter's weather is powered by heat produced deep within the planet. In fact, Jupiter radiates more heat than it receives from the Sun. Jupiter's weather allows scientists to learn about a system totally different from that of Earth. The comparison will help scientists better understand how Earth's weather works.

NASA also made announcements about the nature of Jupiter's rings. Light scattered by particles in the rings revealed the particles were irregularly shaped (as opposed to being round). They likely originate as dust created by the impact of meteorites on some of Jupiter's moons.

6

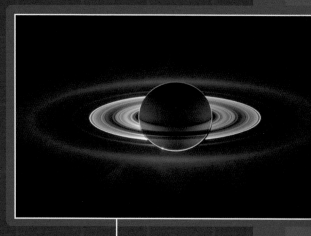

The most fascinating thing about Saturn is, of course, its rings. Seen through even a small telescope, the pale yellow ball and brilliant white rings are one of the most beautiful sights in the sky.

Galileo Galilei first discovered Saturn's rings in 1610, but his telescope wasn't good enough to determine exactly what he was seeing. In 1655 Dutch scientist Christiaan Huygens, using a telescope that was far superior to Galileo's, suggested that Saturn was surrounded by a ring. In 1675 the Italian scientist Giovanni Domenico Cassini found that Saturn's ring was actually made up of many rings with gaps between them. The largest of these gaps was eventually named the Cassini Division.

In 1859 the British physicist James Clerk Maxwell demonstrated that the rings could not be solid or they would become unstable and break apart. Instead, he suggested that the rings were made up of many thousands of small particles, each in its own orbit around Saturn. But just what are those

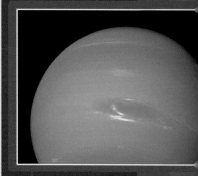

Top: A *Cassini* orbiter view of Saturn and its rings backlit by the Sun. *Center:* Neptune and its clouds as seen from *Voyager 2.* *Bottom:* The takeoff of the booster launching the *Cassini-Huygens* probe to Saturn.

particles? What are they made of? How big are they? Where did they come from? All of these questions had to wait until the first explorers reached the planet.

PIONEER AND VOYAGER

After leaving Jupiter, *Pioneer 11* made a flyby of Saturn on September 1, 1979, at a distance of 13,050 miles (21,000 km) from Saturn's cloud tops. Scientists feared that ring particles might extend far beyond the visible limits of Saturn's rings. These particles might seriously damage a spacecraft zooming through them. Since the Voyager spacecraft were already on their way, NASA made *Pioneer 11* test the

Pioneer 11 took this image as it flew toward Saturn in 1979. The rings are lit from below, which means we are seeing their dark, shadowed side.

route the Voyagers were to follow through the Saturn system. Scientists figured that if *Pioneer 11* did suffer any damage, they could change the course of the Voyagers accordingly by firing their rockets.

Pioneer 11 flew within 21,000 miles (34,000 km) of Saturn's main ring system without a scratch. As it did so, it found two new small moons as well as an additional ring and charted Saturn's magnetic field. It also returned unique photos of Saturn's rings. Since Saturn orbits the Sun far beyond Earth, it is impossible to see the rings with the Sun behind them. *Pioneer 11*, however, was able to swing behind them and, for the first time ever, observe the rings backlit by the Sun. Instead of the familiar bright white bands, the rings looked dark, with thin bright lines.

After a successful gravitational boost from Jupiter, the Voyager spacecraft continued on to Saturn. *Voyager 1* arrived on November 1980, coming within 77,000 miles (124,000 km) of the planet's cloud tops. *Voyager 2* made its closest approach to Saturn on August 25, 1981. Voyager cameras detected unexpectedly complex structures in Saturn's rings. The structures turned out to be made up of thousands of individual, narrow ringlets. Four entirely new rings were discovered, including the mysterious F-ring, which looks like three narrow, stringlike rings braided together.

In addition to studying the ring system, the Voyagers

The twisted F-ring looks like two or three braided strings. The gravity of the small moons distorts the ring and creates this odd appearance.

Voyager 2 sent back this incredible image of Saturn from 21 million miles (34 million km) away. The two small, white dots below the planet are two of Saturn's inner moons. Images such as these were the best ever of Saturn up to that time, revealing much unexpected detail, such as never-before-seen rings.

also examined Saturn itself and many of its moons. One of the moons, Mimas, surprised scientists when photos revealed an enormous crater on its surface nearly one-third as wide as the little moon itself. The crater was named the Deathstar crater because of its resemblance to Darth Vader's space station in the 1977 movie *Star Wars*.

Scientists were particularly eager to get a close look at Saturn's moon Titan, so they decided to abandon the rest of *Voyager 1*'s Grand Tour. Instead, it made a flyby of the mysterious giant moon. Scientists knew Titan had a dense atmosphere, which *Voyager 1* revealed to be made up mostly of nitrogen and methane. It has a surface pressure 1.6 times that of Earth at sea level. But Titan turned out to be much colder than some scientists expected. In fact, it is too cold for life to exist.

Still, *Voyager 1* gave scientists only an enticing glimpse of Titan. It didn't show them anything on the surface. Titan turned out to be covered with an opaque layer of clouds, much like Venus. Photos the spacecraft sent back showed a nearly featureless orange ball. Although scientists knew that the surface beneath those clouds is very cold, no one knew what kind of landscape was there. They had to wait nearly twenty-five years to find out.

VOYAGER 2 MEETS URANUS

After getting a boost from the gravity of Saturn, *Voyager 2* continued on into the outer solar system. The first planet it encountered after Saturn was Uranus. Uranus is distinguished by the fact that it is tipped 97 degrees onto its side. Astronomers think its unusual position is the result of a collision with a planet-sized body early in the solar system's history. Something, perhaps another planet, hit Uranus so hard that it literally knocked the giant planet sideways.

Voyager 2's closest approach to Uranus occurred on January 24, 1986. It came within 50,600 miles (81,500 km) of the planet's cloud tops. When *Voyager 2* arrived, it found that Uranus was a virtually featureless blue sphere—like a large, blank, blue balloon. The lack of features is probably due to the intense cold. The planet lacks enough energy to create the colorful storms visible in the atmospheres of Jupiter and Saturn. While flying past the planet, *Voyager 2*

In 1986 *Voyager 2* reached Uranus. Its photos revealed that the planet is a blank, blue ball.

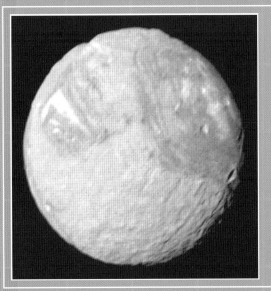

The tiny moon Miranda was once shattered into pieces when another body collided with it. Eventually, the pieces of Miranda came back together due to the pull of their mutual gravity. The moon ended up looking like a broken cup badly glued back together.

discovered ten previously unknown moons around Uranus. The ten new moons brought the total number of moons known at that time to fifteen. Most of them are very small, with the largest measuring only about 90 miles (150 km) in diameter.

The moon Miranda, innermost of the five large moons, revealed itself to be one of the strangest bodies yet seen in the solar system. Detailed images from *Voyager 2*'s flyby showed huge canyons as deep as 12 miles (20 km), terraced layers, and a mixture of old and young surfaces. Miranda looks very much as though it had been broken and then badly reassembled. The current theory suggests that this is exactly what may have happened. Millions of years ago, Miranda may have been impacted by a body large enough to literally shatter it. The pieces went into orbit around Uranus and were eventually drawn back together by their mutual gravity.

Voyager 2 also studied the rings of Uranus—which Earth-based observers had previously discovered. The rings proved to be very different from Jupiter's thin dusty bands and Saturn's bright icy ones. They are very black and may be made of carbonaceous particles (material with high carbon content).

VOYAGER 2 VISITS NEPTUNE

Voyager 2 made its closest approach to Neptune on August 25, 1989. Images returned to Earth showed more cloud details than Uranus had as well as a set of partial rings. The images also revealed several new moons.

Voyager 2 showed a huge, dark blue oval feature in Neptune's clouds. NASA scientists named it the Great Dark Spot, but it has since disappeared. It may have been a vast, cyclonic storm system similar to the Great Red Spot of Jupiter.

Since Neptune was the last major planet *Voyager 2* could visit, NASA decided to make a close flyby of the moon Triton, even though the gravitational sling of Triton would throw the spacecraft out of the solar system forever. Triton turned out to have a fascinating surface, covered

 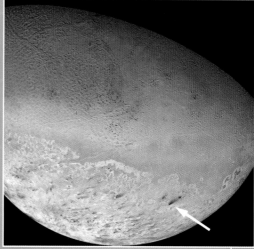

Voyager 1 took this portrait *(left)* of cloud-covered Neptune during its flyby of the planet in 1989. The probe discovered a frigid world covered in blue clouds and streaked by high, wispy white clouds. The oval-shaped dark blue spot is a huge storm similar to the Great Red Spot on Jupiter. *Voyager 2* took many images of Neptune's giant moon Triton, including the one above *(right)* showing its icy surface. The tiny dark smudges (indicated by the arrow) are deposits left on the ground by ice volcanoes blasting material high above the surface.

with dark, fan-shaped deposits from huge ice volcanoes. Ice volcanoes don't contain lava. Instead, they have huge eruptions of cold liquids and gases. Powered by heat generated deep within the Moon's crust—much like the volcanoes of Io—these areas may be warm enough to support some form of life. It was surprising to find such features on a world that scientists had thought far too cold to have any active geology.

Voyager 2's encounter with Triton sent it on a course down and out of the solar system. In about 358,000 years, it will pass within 0.8 light years of the star Sirius. Although it is still sending weak signals, its power source will have long gone dead by the time it reaches that distant star.

CASSINI-HUYGENS

The European Space Agency and NASA developed a joint mission called Cassini-Huygens to further explore Saturn. Launched in October 1987, it consisted of two spacecraft: *Cassini*, which would go into orbit around Saturn, and *Huygens*, which would make a soft landing on Saturn's giant moon, Titan.

WHO WERE CASSINI AND HUYGENS?

Giovanni Domenico Cassini (1625–1712) was an Italian scientist and engineer. He was an astronomer at the Panzano Observatory and a professor of astronomy at the University of Bologna. In 1671 he became director of the Paris Observatory. He discovered, along with Robert Hooke, Jupiter's Great Red Spot around 1665. He was also first to observe four of Saturn's moons. In 1675 he discovered the broad gap in Saturn's rings that came to be known as the Cassini Division.

Christiaan Huygens (1629–1695) was a Dutch mathematician and physicist. He discovered Saturn's largest moon, Titan, in 1655. He also studied Saturn's rings and in 1656 determined that they had to consist of tiny individual particles.

A MESSAGE TO THE STARS

Like *Pioneer 10* and *11*, the two Voyager spacecraft carried a message from Earth. NASA attached a gold-plated phonograph record to each spacecraft. Each record contains encoded sounds, voices, music, and images reflecting the diversity of life and culture on Earth. Each spacecraft eventually left the solar system and entered interstellar space—the space between the stars, far beyond the domain of the Sun. So there is a possibility that someday—perhaps thousands of years in the future—beings from some other star system might discover this relic of Earth and humankind. They might learn what we and our various cultures were like.

Carl Sagan chaired the committee that selected the contents of the records for NASA. Sagan and his associates assembled 115 images and a variety of natural sounds. The sounds included those made by surf, wind, and thunder, as well as animal sounds, including the songs of birds and whales. They also added ninety minutes of musical selections from different cultures and eras, ranging from tribal music to classical pieces to rhythm and blues. They even included spoken greetings in fifty-five languages as well as printed messages from former U.S. president Jimmy Carter and UN secretary-general Kurt Waldheim.

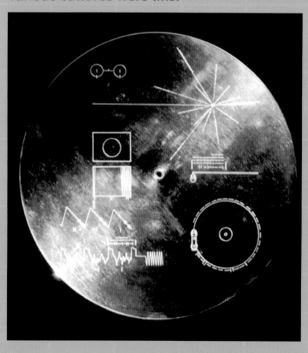

The golden record carried aboard *Pioneer 10* and *Pioneer 11* showed mathematical and astronomical symbols indicating the location of Earth in the galaxy. The other side contained an audio-video recording of 115 different sounds from Earth. It also held images of people, places, and animals; music; and spoken greetings in fifty-five languages.

Scientists created this spectacular image of Saturn by combining a total of 165 images taken by *Cassini*'s wide-angle camera over nearly three hours on September 15, 2006. The Sun is directly behind the planet, so Saturn and its rings are backlit. The faint bluish ring circling the planet is the E-ring, which is composed mostly of material ejected from the ice fountains on the Saturn moon named Enceladus.

Even before arriving in the Saturn system, the spacecraft discovered two new moons of Saturn. They are both very small. Scientists named them Methone and Pallene. In May 2005, *Cassini* discovered another new moon within one of the gaps in Saturn's rings. Astronomers named it Daphnis. A moon named Pan is the only other moon known to orbit inside Saturn's ring system.

On June 11, 2004, *Cassini* made a close flyby of Saturn's moon Phoebe. This was the first opportunity for close-up studies of this moon since the *Voyager 2* flyby. *Cassini* showed evidence that bright patches on the surface of the heavily cratered moon might be underground ice that has been exposed by meteorite impacts.

On July 1, 2004, after a seven-year journey, *Cassini* flew through a gap in the thin outermost ring and entered orbit around

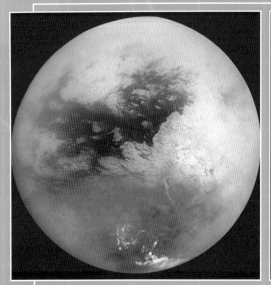 

The surface of Titan is not visible from space because it is covered by a thick blanket of yellow orange clouds. The radar on board the *Cassini* orbiter, however, is able to penetrate those clouds, allowing scientists a glimpse of the surface that lies beneath *(left)*. The radar does not take an actual photo of the surface. Instead, it indicates which areas are rough and which are smooth. The light regions are probably hills, mountains, and plains. The dark, smooth areas may be large lakes and seas of liquid methane. The small patch of white near the bottom is clouds near the south pole. *Right: Cassini* made a major discovery when it revealed the existence of geysers on Enceladus, one of Saturn's many moons. The faint gray plume extending below the moon is gas and other materials being vented from these geysers.

Saturn—the first spacecraft ever to do so. Only a day later, *Cassini* made its first distant flyby of Saturn's largest moon, Titan. It approached within 211,000 miles (339,000 km) and took images through special filters able to see through the dense haze that covers the moon. The images showed south polar clouds thought to be composed of methane and surface features with widely differing brightness. On closer passes, radar imagery revealed that much of the surface of Titan was relatively flat, with surface features no more than 150 feet (50 m) high.

Cassini also made flybys of the moon Enceladus, discovering that it has a thin atmosphere of water vapor. It showed enormous water ice geysers erupting from the south polar region. Scientists speculate that these may be fueled by underground pockets of water, making Enceladus one of the few bodies in our solar system known to have liquid water.

HUYGENS

The second part of the *Cassini-Huygens* spacecraft was the *Huygens* probe. NASA designed *Huygens* to enter Titan's atmosphere and parachute a robotic laboratory down to the surface. Since the surface of Titan is invisible from Earth, *Cassini* had to examine the surface with its radar to find a safe landing site for *Huygens*.

The first part of the mission was a parachute descent through Titan's atmosphere on January 18, 2005. The lander's batteries could only last for 153 minutes, allowing for a maximum descent time of 2.5 hours plus three additional minutes to half an hour on Titan's surface. Scientists say the lander appears to have landed on the shoreline of a large lake, complete with islands and

THE *HUYGENS* PROBE

The *Huygens* probe system consists of two parts. The 700-pound (318 kg) probe descended to Titan. The probe support equipment remained attached to the orbiting spacecraft. The support equipment included the electronics necessary to track the probe, recover the data gathered during its descent, and process and deliver the data to the orbiter. The orbiter then transmitted the data back to Earth. The probe's instruments measured temperature and determined the composition of Titan's atmosphere. Cameras took views of the surface while the probe descended and while it was on the surface.

The *Huygens* lander touched down on the mysterious moon Titan in January 2005 and took the first photo of its surface. The photo revealed an orange-sherbet-colored surface made mostly of ice. What appear to be rocks are actually chunks of ice— mostly frozen water and methane. The color comes from the presence of hydrocarbons. These are organic compounds containing only carbon and hydrogen. They are created when ultraviolet light from the Sun causes reactions among the water, methane, and other molecules in Titan's upper atmosphere. Similar organic molecules give Jupiter its red, orange, and yellow colors.

drainage channels winding into it from the mainland. Photos taken on the surface show fist-sized chunks of water ice scattered over an orange surface, which seems to be a claylike material with a thin crust.

Although the lake that *Huygens* landed near appears to be dry at the moment, recent radar images obtained by *Cassini* seem to show lakes of liquid hydrocarbons—perhaps liquid methane—in Titan's southern latitudes. This is the first discovery of currently existing lakes anywhere besides Earth. The lakes range in size from about 0.6 miles (1 km) to 62 miles (100) wide.

Although Titan is too cold for life as we know it, it might have places on its surface where life might have evolved. One of the most exciting discoveries is the existence of thermal features—such as springs, geysers, and ice volcanoes—on the surface of Titan.

7

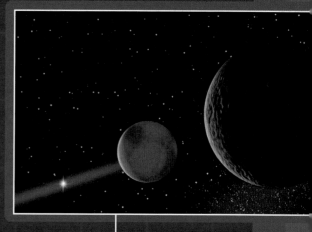

Mercury and Pluto lie at the two extremes of the solar system. Mercury is a tiny world that orbits closer to the Sun than any other planet. Pluto is an icy body at the very frontier of the solar system. Pluto is so far away that the Sun appears to be nothing but an especially bright star. The Sun is too far away to provide the planet with much heat.

Details about Pluto are shrouded from view by sheer distance. But Mercury is hard to see not only because it is so small but also because it is very close to the Sun. Until the first space probes visited it, Mercury was almost as big a mystery as distant Pluto.

MERCURY

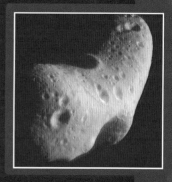

Spacecraft visited Mercury for the first time in 1974 when *Mariner 10* made three flybys. *Mariner 10* had already flown past Venus. The encounter with Venus's gravity deflected the course of the probe and caused it to slow down, sending it on a path toward the Sun. On its first pass by Mercury,

Top: An artist's impression of Pluto *(right)* and its moon, Charon *(center)*. *Center:* An artist's impression of the *Stardust* space-craft approaching a comet named Wild 2. *Bottom:* The asteroid Eros in one of the hundreds of photos taken by *NEAR Shoemaker* orbiter.

Mariner 10 approached to within 430 miles (690 km) of the planet. After making its first flyby, *Mariner 10* orbited around the Sun and passed by the planet two more times, each encounter about six months apart.

The pictures *Mariner 10* sent to Earth revealed a planet that looked very much like our own Moon. Mercury is heavily cratered. Unlike the Moon, it has huge cliffs, or scarps, that run for long distances across the surface, often slicing right through older features such as craters. Some of these craters may be cracks caused by the impact of the huge asteroid that created Mare Caloris, an 808-mile-wide (1,300-km) feature that looks like an enormous bulls-eye.

Mariner 10 photographed less than half the planet. So scientists still have much to learn about its surface. NASA sent a new robotic mission called *Mercury Messenger* to Mercury in August 2004. Instruments have improved vastly in the past thirty years. Scientists should be able to learn a great deal more about Mercury than the basic information *Mariner 10* discovered.

Mariner 10 sent back views of the rugged, sunbaked surface of the planet Mercury. They revealed a heavily cratered world not unlike our own Moon.

Scientists created this overall view of the planet Mercury by assembling many smaller photos taken by the *Mercury Messenger* spacecraft.

Mercury Messenger will make three flybys of the planet and then go into orbit in 2011 for a yearlong study of Mercury. Among other duties, it will create the first detailed map of Mercury. Other instruments will measure the thickness of the planet's crust and determine whether Mercury has any sort of atmosphere. *Messenger* will also look for any ice that may lie in the shaded craters of the north and south poles.

THE FRONTIER OF THE SOLAR SYSTEM

Discovered in 1930, Pluto was long considered by scientists to be the farthest planet from the Sun. It is forty times farther from the Sun than Earth. Pluto is a tiny world, only 1,400 miles (2,253 km) across—approximately half the width of the United States. Scientists don't even know exactly what Pluto looks like, other than that it is pinkish and has dark and light patches. They do know that it is made almost entirely of ice.

Pluto is one of the largest bodies in the Kuiper belt. This region, named after astrophysicist Gerard Kuiper, holds small icy bodies beyond the orbit of Neptune. These ice dwarfs are ancient relics that formed over 4 billion years ago. They are about 124 miles to 1,240 miles (200 to 2,000 km) wide, much smaller than the full-grown rocky and gas giant planets.

Pluto *(right)* and its moon Charon orbit at the very frontier of the solar system. As planet-sized members of the Kuiper belt, they are icy worlds that may be part of the debris left over from the formation of the solar system.

Because the larger planets may have started as ice dwarfs, ice dwarfs have a great deal to teach us about planetary formation. Scientists believe that the solar system formed from a vast cloud of dust and gas. This cloud eventually began to draw together under the effect of its own gravity, forming tiny grains of matter. The grains came together—in a process called accretion—to form even larger grains and then large clumps. Eventually, many of these clumps grew to become the planets we know. Scientists think that most of the bodies in the Kuiper belt are samples of the original clumps of matter that formed the planets—like a pile of bricks left over from building a house. Studying this original material will help scientists understand how our own Earth formed.

The Kuiper belt is also the major source of the comets that have impacted Earth. One such impact, 65 million years ago, may have caused the extinction of the dinosaurs. (Scientists think that dust was thrown into Earth's atmosphere and changed the climate by shielding the surface of Earth from the Sun.) By cataloging the various-sized craters on Pluto, its moon Charon, and other Kuiper belt objects, scientists may be able to estimate the number of large cometary bodies lurking in the outer solar system.

In 2006 the International Astronomical Union changed the definition of the word *planet*. As a result, Pluto was reclassified as a dwarf planet (though many astronomers disagree with the new definition of planet). Nevertheless, Pluto and it three moons remain an exciting destination for space probes. NASA launched the first such probe, *New Horizons*, in January 2006.

New Horizons will be the first spacecraft to explore Pluto, its moon Charon, and the Kuiper belt. Traveling at 36,300 miles per hour (58,418 km/h) , the probe is the fastest spacecraft ever launched from Earth. It passed the Moon only five hours after launch. But it will still take nearly ten years to reach the distant little world. In February 2007, *New Horizons* passed through the Jupiter system at 47,000 miles per hour (75,637 km/h) to get a slingshot gravity assist from the giant planet.

When *New Horizons* finally reaches Pluto in July 2015, it will begin close-up observations of the dwarf planet. (Some instruments will start gathering data up to six months earlier.) Long-range imaging of Pluto and Charon will begin 3.2 days from the closest encounter and will be able to detect features as small as 25 miles (40 km). Coverage will be repeated twice per day to search for changes due to ice volcanoes, if they exist there.

During and after the closest approach, *New Horizon*'s cameras should be able to see details as small as 60 feet (20 m) across. Other

THE STAMP THAT HELPED LAUNCH A SPACE MISSION

In 1991 the U.S. Postal Service issued a set of ten commemorative stamps honoring some of the many different space probes that had explored the solar system up to that time. There was one for each planet—and the Moon—showing the spacecraft associated with exploring it. Pluto's stamp had to bear the legend "Not Yet Explored," because no space probe had been sent there yet.

A great many scientists had wanted to send a space probe to Pluto and several missions had already been proposed. Having a stamp declaring to the world that humans had explored all the major worlds of the solar system but one was not only embarrassing, scientists saw it as a kind of challenge. In January 2006, the *New Horizons* probe was finally launched on its ten-year-long journey toward Pluto. The probe carried one of the Pluto postage stamps with it, in recognition of the inspiration the unexplored planet had provided.

PLUTO NOT YET EXPLORED **29** USA

instruments will measure Pluto's temperature and atmosphere and search for possible rings around the planet.

After passing by Pluto, *New Horizons* will continue farther into the Kuiper belt. Mission planners are searching for one or more large Kuiper belt objects for flybys similar to the spacecraft's encounter with Pluto.

ENCOUNTERS WITH COMETS

The Kuiper belt is one of the main sources of the comets that occasionally enter the inner solar system. For more than a century, scientists have wanted to study these samples from the farthest outskirts of the solar system. But comets are not very large—only a few miles across—and they travel very fast once they reach the inner solar system. Also, as they get close to the Sun, the ice they contain warms up and turns to gas, hiding the comet itself behind a glowing veil. This makes it very difficult for scientists to study the mysterious comets from Earth.

In 1910, when Halley's comet passed by Earth, astronomers had only telescopes and cameras with which to study it. In 1986 Halley's comet returned to the vicinity of Earth for the first time in seventy-six years. A fleet of five spacecraft from Earth was waiting for it, all intent on discovering its secrets. Japan, the Soviet Union, and the European Space Agency had all sent probes. The United States had to back out due to lack of funding. (NASA, however, discovered that a U.S. probe orbiting the Sun could be redirected to intercept another comet—Giacobini-Zimmer. The probe passed through the tail of this comet in 1985, the first spacecraft to ever have direct contact with a comet.)

The Japanese *Sakigake* and *Suisei* probes made passes near Halley's comet. The Soviet

In 1986 ESA's *Giotto* space probe took the first close-up photo of a comet's nucleus. This image of Halley's comet revealed that the surface of the nucleus was coal black, with Sun-warmed gas shooting away in bright jets.

Vega 1 and *Vega 2* probes (following their contacts with Venus) came within 5,600 miles (9,000 km) of the comet's nucleus—the dark, icy body hidden behind the glowing tail. The most successful of the five probes was ESA's *Giotto*, which approached to within 375 miles (600 km) of the nucleus. It sent back valuable data as well as pictures, including the first-ever close-up images of a comet's nucleus. The photos revealed a surprisingly dark (almost coal black), peanut-shaped body measuring 5 by 5 by 10 miles (8 by 8 by 16 km), with bright jets shooting from its surface. A glowing fog surrounded the entire comet.

The coma (the cloud of glowing dust and gas surrounding a comet) around the nucleus was so filled with dust and debris that *Giotto* may have picked up more than 20 pounds (12 kg) of cometary material as it passed through. *Giotto* managed to determine the makeup of the gases surrounding the comet. Nearly 20 tons (18 metric tons) of gas streamed from the nucleus every second. The gas makeup was 80 percent water, 10 percent carbon monoxide, and traces of carbon dioxide, ammonia, methane, and hydrocyanic acid.

Touching a Comet

NASA launched *Stardust* on February 7, 1999. Stardust was the first U.S. space mission dedicated solely to exploring a comet. It was also the first robotic mission designed to return extraterrestrial material from outside the orbit of the Moon. Its primary goal was to collect dust and carbon-based samples during its closest encounter with comet Wild 2 in January 2004.

To rendezvous with Wild 2, *Stardust* made three loops around the Sun. On the second loop, its trajectory intersected that of the comet. *Stardust* flew through at least two large jets of debris during its approach to comet Wild 2. Using a substance called aerogel, *Stardust* captured samples of the gas and dust surrounding the comet's nucleus, keeping them safely embedded for return to Earth.

Stardust also photographed an image of the comet's nucleus that revealed overlapping pits and depressions where material had boiled off in the past. The black-and-white navigation camera image showed a huge pit as large as a dozen football stadiums, along with at least five active gas jets. A comet is composed mainly of ice made of frozen gases. As the comet approaches the Sun, the ice warms up, just as an ice cube would on a sidewalk on a sunny day. As the ice turns back into gas, it streams away from the surface of the comet in huge, geyserlike jets.

After a seven-year, 3-billion-mile (5-billion-km) journey in space, *Stardust* returned to Earth in January 2006. A canister containing the samples it had gathered survived reentry into Earth's atmosphere. But the parachute meant to slow its landing failed, and the canister crashed into the Utah desert. Fortunately, when the panicked scientists were finally able to examine the contents, they discovered that much of it was intact.

The comet samples are expected to be made up of the ancient grains of matter that were formed during the birth of the solar system. Studying this material will give scientists important clues about the origin of the solar system and perhaps even the origins of life.

An artist's impression shows the *Stardust* spacecraft meeting comet Wild 2 in 2004.

The Stardust mission successfully recovered some of the dust from the tail of comet Wild 2 and returned the samples to Earth. This is a microscopic view of one of the tiny dust grains that compose a comet's tail. These materials are believed to consist of ancient interstellar grains that include remnants from the formation of the solar system. Studying this material will give important insights into the evolution of the Sun, the planets, and possibly even the origins of life itself.

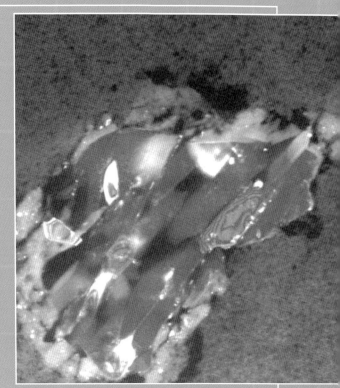

DEEP IMPACT

Scientists didn't simply want to study the gases and dust flowing from a comet. They wanted to know what the nucleus itself was like. What materials made up its surface, and what lay beneath? To learn more, NASA created the *Deep Impact* probe.

Following its launch on January 12, 2005, *Deep Impact* traveled nearly 27 million miles (43 million km) in 174 days to reach the comet Tempel 1. Once the spacecraft reached the vicinity of the comet on July 3, 2005, it separated into two portions, an impactor and a flyby probe. The impactor used its thrusters to move into the path of the comet, hitting it head-on twenty-four hours later at a speed of 23,000 miles per hour (37,000 km/h).

The impactor, a mass of 814 pounds (370 kg) of solid copper, exploded with a force equal to 4.5 tons (4 metric tons) of TNT. Scientists believe that the energy of this high-velocity collision was sufficient to

When *Deep Impact* reached the comet Tempel 1, it launched a coffee-table-sized impactor weighing 23,000 pounds (10,433 kg). When the impactor hit the comet, it created the huge explosion shown here. The materials blown out from deep within the comet allowed scientists to study the interior of a comet for the first time.

create a crater up to 300 feet (100 m) wide—larger than the arena of the Coliseum in Rome. They were trying to discover what materials the comet was made of—especially materials that existed deep below its outer crust. The explosion of the impactor blew material from beneath the surface into space, where the flyby probe could analyze it.

Just minutes after the impact, the flyby probe came within 310 miles (500 km) of the nucleus. It took pictures of the crater location, the plume of material ejected by the explosion, and the entire cometary nucleus. Scientists around the world photographed the event with Earth-based telescopes and orbital observatories, including the Hubble Space Telescope. Cameras and spectroscopes on board the European Space Agency's *Rosetta* spacecraft, which was about 50 million miles (80 million km) from the comet, also observed the impact. *Rosetta*'s instruments will help analyze the material blown from the comet.

Scientists are still analyzing data from the mission, but initial results have been surprising. The material excavated by the impact con-tained more dust and less ice than scientists expected. In addition, the material was finer than expected. Scientists likened it to powder rather than sand. They were disappointed that the impact did not seem to have penetrated below the upper layer of material. Many scientists felt that it had only scratched the surface.

Analysis of data from the Swift X-ray telescope showed that the crater continued to spew gases for thirteen days, with a peak five days after impact. The comet ejected a total of 250,000 tons (227,000 metric tons) of water.

PROBES MEET THE ASTEROIDS

Scientists once considered asteroids to be mere debris cluttering up the solar system. But modern scientists believe they are very important. They may give us clues about the origins of the solar system and the way in which planets form. They may also be valuable future resources for metals and other materials. And, finally, the likelihood of a future impact such as the one that wiped out the dinosaurs makes understanding asteroids even more important.

Galileo was the first spacecraft to make close flybys of asteroids, photographing Gaspra and Ida while on its way to Jupiter. But Near Earth Asteroid Rendezvous (NEAR) Shoemaker was the first spacecraft mission specifically designed to study an asteroid. The objective of the mission was to rendezvous with a near-Earth asteroid named Eros. The craft would orbit it for a year, collecting imagery and gathering data on the asteroid's surface features, composition, and rotation. (Originally named *NEAR*, the spacecraft was renamed *NEAR Shoemaker* in honor of the late Eugene Shoemaker, a renowned planetary scientist, after arriving at the asteroid.)

NASA launched *NEAR Shoemaker* on February 17, 1996, and sent it on a four-year journey to 433 Eros. On its way to Eros, *NEAR Shoemaker* encountered asteroid 253 Mathilde. It revealed that the tiny asteroid—36 by 29 miles (59 by 47 km)—had been a victim of many impacts. One large crater is estimated to be nearly 6 miles (10 km) deep.

NAMING ASTEROIDS

Planets and moons are named following fairly strict rules set up by the international community of astronomers. But asteroids can have almost any name their discoverer chooses. Scientists gave the earliest asteroids the names of Greek and Roman gods and goddesses, just like the planets. Ceres was the first, then Pallas, Eros, and others.

But as astronomers began to discover hundreds of asteroids, they ran out of mythological names. They started naming asteroids after historical figures, famous scientists, characters from books and, eventually, friends and family. Asteroids have even been named for cities, rock stars, and television and movie characters. One asteroid is called Mr. Spock, for instance, and another is called James Bond. The asteroid Ekard is the name of Drake University spelled backward.

Asteroids also have a number attached to their name. These numbers are given in the order they are discovered. The full proper name of Ceres, for instance, is 1 Ceres and that of Eros is 433 Eros. But the number is usually dropped when it's a well-known asteroid. If an asteroid is not given a name by its discoverer, it is known by its number, year of discovery, and special code letters. The unnamed asteroid (3360) 1981 VA is an example. This tells astronomers that it was the 3,360th asteroid to be discovered and that it was first seen in 1981. Nearly 158,000 asteroids have been discovered, and nearly 14,000 have been given names.

NEAR Shoemaker finally reached Eros on February 14, 2000. It photographed the asteroid from altitudes ranging from 200 miles (320 km) to as low as 3 miles (5 km). The spacecraft successfully completed its mission in February 2001, when it carried out a previously unplanned landing. This was the first time a spacecraft ever landed on an asteroid. The landing wasn't done for any special scientific reason. (In fact, the spacecraft wasn't even designed for a landing.) Its operators simply wanted to see if it could be done.

HAYABUSA

The Japanese Aerospace Exploration Agency launched the asteroid probe *Hayabusa* (a Japanese word meaning "falcon") in May 2003. *Hayabusa* was the first spacecraft purposely designed to land on an asteroid. Its mission was to collect a sample of material from the small near-Earth asteroid 25143 Itokawa and return the sample to Earth for further analysis. The *Hayabusa* mission, if successful, will mark the first time that an asteroid sample has been returned to Earth.

Hayabusa took two years to reach Itokawa. Once in orbit around Itokawa, *Hayabusa* studied its shape, rotation, topography, color, composition, and density. Finally, in November 2005, it successfully landed on the asteroid, where it collected samples to return to Earth. After briefly touching the surface in order to pick up a sample, the spacecraft quickly moved away. *Hayabusa* made several more brief landings, each time collecting samples. The longest time it ever spent on the surface of the asteroid was half an hour.

During *Hayabusa*'s second landing, it fired tiny projectiles into the asteroid's surface. Scientists hoped that it would be able to catch the resulting spray of material, which would give them some idea of the material that lay beneath the surface. This material would be held in a separate capsule to return to Earth. Unfortunately, no one knows if the projectiles actually fired. Like many spacecraft that operate so far from Earth, *Hayabusa* depended on decisions made by its on-board computer. Scientists will have to wait to see if there is anything in the container when it finally returns to Earth in 2010.

When *Hayabusa* is about 186,000 to 250,000 miles (300,000 to 400,000 km) from Earth, the reentry capsule will detach from the main unit. The capsule will then reenter Earth's atmosphere. If all goes well, it will land by parachute near Woomera, Australia, in June 2010.

8

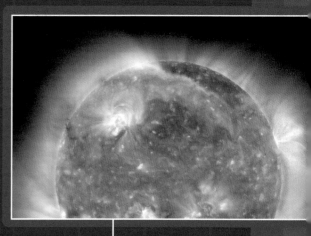

The solar system has more than just planets and moons for scientists to explore. There is, of course, the Sun, but there is also interplanetary space itself. What lies between the planets? You might at first think the answer is nothing. But space is filled with all kinds of atomic particles and radiation. Most of it is pouring from the Sun and bathing the planets—Earth included—like the currents of an enormous, invisible ocean rushing past scattered islands.

Scientists have sent many probes into interplanetary space to study the environment in which Earth orbits. Two of the first U.S. satellites, *Explorer 1* and *Explorer 3*, made significant findings about the mysterious cosmic rays (radiation from deep space) that bombard Earth. These findings led to the discovery of the Van Allen radiation belts that surround Earth.

While on their way to the Moon, Soviet space probes *Luna 1, 2,* and *3* and the U.S. probe *Pioneer 4* discovered an

Top: The Sun as viewed in infrared light by the *SOHO* spacecraft. *Center:* An artist's impression of the future *Phoenix* Mars lander. *Bottom:* In the future, robotic missions to Mars will send samples back to Earth in rockets such as this one.

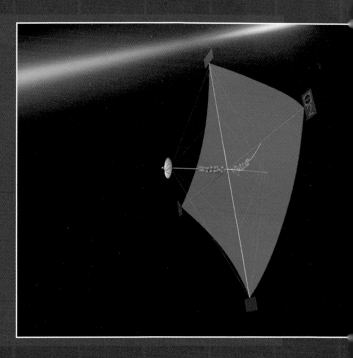

An artist's impression shows the solar sail spacecraft proposed by NASA. It would navigate by the pressure of the solar wind—a constant stream of atomic particles emitted by the Sun—just like a sailing ship is propelled by Earth's wind. Solar wind does not create much force, but over time it will add up to great speeds. Solar sails are appealing to NASA because they could be very cheap, requiring no fuel.

entirely unexpected phenomenon: the existence of the solar wind. This is not really wind as on Earth. Rather it is a stream of atomic particles thrown out from the Sun at speeds of 200 to 350 miles per second (300 to 550 km/s). Future spacecraft may take advantage of this wind by using sails just as seafarers once did on the oceans of Earth. These spacecraft would have a sail consisting of a very thin, lightweight plastic. Because the solar wind is so thin, the sail will have to be huge—the size of several football fields. A solar sailing spacecraft requires no fuel, so it may be the best choice for missions to the outer planets that may take many years. As long as the Sun shines, the solar sail will keep working.

These discoveries inspired a long series of space probes launched specifically to study the Sun and its environment—too many, in fact, to describe in detail. A number of particularly outstanding missions, however, have taught us a great deal about our personal star.

THE SUN

The Orbiting Solar Observatories (OSO) are some of the earliest and most important among the many solar probes NASA has launched. Beginning in 1962, NASA successfully sent seven OSO into orbit to study solar flares, ultraviolet, X-ray, and gamma ray radiation, and the solar corona (the glowing outer atmosphere of the Sun).

The first space probe investigations near the Sun began with Helios, a German-American collaboration. Two probes, *Helios 1* and *Helios 2*, were launched successfully in 1974 and 1976. These probes were to approach the Sun as near as possible in order to find out how it affects both Earth and nearby space.

Scientists have long known that the Sun does not emit energy always at the same rate. The amount of heat and light coming from the Sun changes even from day to day. Discovering irregularities in solar radiation and the forces that cause them is important to life on Earth. Many phenomena in nature can be attributed to varying solar radiation. The sunspot cycle—in which the number of sunspots dramatically increases every eleven years, for instance—influences the world's climate. The solar wind causes auroras (the effect of electrically charged particles from the Sun striking the upper atmosphere of Earth) in the polar regions.

Helios 1 and *2* approached the Sun as close as 31 million miles (50 million km), about a third the distance of Earth from the Sun (roughly the distance of Mercury). They are shaped like double cones whose surfaces are covered with special mirrors. Their solar cells generate electricity. Helios rotates about once every second to distribute heat evenly, like a chicken on a rotisserie. Despite this, the surfaces of the probes were heated to temperatures of several hundred degrees. Nevertheless, they survived these harsh conditions without damage and are still sending data to Earth after more than thirty years.

The probes take about 190 days to make one orbit around the Sun. Each one is equipped with several experiments. Among these are instruments that analyze the subatomic particles making up the solar wind and record their speed, direction, and number. They also contain magnetometers that measure the permanent magnetic field of the Sun and the gradual changes that occur in it. The probes also have instruments for measuring the electrical field that surrounds the Sun. Three photometers measure the brightness of the sky in different directions.

SOHO

The *Solar and Heliospheric Observatory* (*SOHO*), a joint ESA/NASA project, is stationed nearly 1 million miles (1.5 million km) from Earth. *SOHO* orbits on the sunward side of Earth in a region of space called Lagrange point L1. This spot is where the gravitational fields of Earth and the Sun balance each other, keeping *SOHO* in a stable orbit.

SOHO has a permanently unobstructed view of the Sun. It constantly watches the Sun, returning spectacular pictures and data about the storms raging across its surface. Every day *SOHO* transmits images taken in several different colors of light. These images tell scientists a great deal about the nature of the Sun and its behavior. The information can help predict solar events that affect our planet.

SOHO studies the Sun's hot interior through its visible surface and stormy atmosphere. It also studies distant regions where the wind from the Sun meets a breeze of atoms coming from the stars. Where they meet is called the heliopause. The point where the solar wind is slowed down and eventually stopped by the incoming wind from the stars marks the point where interstellar space begins.

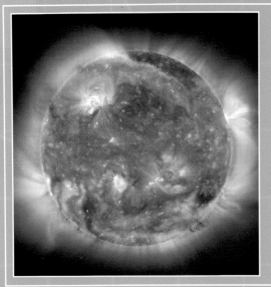

SOHO can see the Sun in wavelengths of light that are invisible to the human eye. This image, created in 1998, combines several views taken in infrared light. It reveals detailed features that cannot be seen in ordinary light.

SOHO has discovered complex currents of gas flowing beneath the visible solar surface and rapid changes in the pattern of magnetic fields. In the Sun's atmosphere, *SOHO* has seen explosions, huge shock waves, and even vast cyclonic storms.

Beyond the Solar System

Only four spacecraft have ever left the solar system entirely. Although it was not part of their original mission, the Pioneer and Voyager spacecraft have sent back valuable information about what lies in interstellar space.

After its successful flyby of Jupiter, *Pioneer 10* continued to gather scientific data about the outer regions of the solar system until the end of its mission in March 1997. However, the Deep Space Network, a worldwide array of antennae NASA maintains, continued to track *Pioneer 10*'s weak signal. It received the last signal from *Pioneer 10* on January 23, 2003.

After leaving Saturn, *Pioneer 11* explored the outer regions of the solar system, studying the solar wind and cosmic rays. This work finally ended in September 1995, when power levels became too low to run the instruments. At that time, the spacecraft was located at 4,157,100,000 miles (6,705,000,000 km) from the Sun. It was heading toward the constellation of Aquila, northwest of the constellation of Sagittarius. *Pioneer 11* will pass near one of the stars in Aquila in about 4 million years.

As *Voyager 1* headed into interstellar space after its encounter with Saturn, its instruments continued to study the solar system. Scientists have been using the probe to search for the heliopause, which is the ultimate frontier of the solar system. Scientists think *Voyager 1* will cross that line in the year 2015.

In November 2005, *Voyager 1* reached a distance of 9.05 billion miles (14.6 billion km)—ninety-seven times farther from the Sun than Earth. This is the farthest from Earth any human-made object has ever traveled. At this distance, a signal from Earth takes nearly 13.8 hours to reach the spacecraft. As of July 2006, *Voyager 2* was eighty times farther from the Sun than Earth, placing it well beyond Pluto.

THE FUTURE

More and more robotic space probes are being planned every year. They continue to prove their value in exploring space effectively and cheaply. Scientists and engineers—and the politicians who must approve their budgets—have come to realize that many robotic probes can be launched for the same cost as a single space shuttle flight.

NASA is planning probes for future missions to Mars. These pilotless aircraft and balloons will be able to carry instruments and cameras anywhere on the Martian surface. NASA is also planning probes that will drill deep into the Martian soil. More sophisticated and elaborate rovers will be able to travel many miles across the landscape.

An artist's impression shows the *Phoenix* lander that NASA hopes to send to Mars in the near future. The lander is specially designed to look for water and signs of past or present life on the planet.

One of NASA's most unusual ideas is the release of a swarm of probes, each the size of a baseball, that would spread across Mars in every direction. Thousands of electrically powered probes could cover a vast area currently beyond the reach of modern rovers. These little probes could explore remote and rocky terrain that large rovers cannot navigate. They could carry many different types of sensors, including cameras. The tiny, 4-ounce (100-gram) probes could also make their way into cracks, crevices, and caves that rovers cannot reach.

Artificial muscles inside the probes could allow them to hop an average of six times an hour, traveling about 5 feet (1.5 m) each time. A swarm of probes could cover 50 square miles (129 sq. km) in a month. A big advantage to the plan is that if a few probes out of the hundreds or thousands were lost, the mission could still be highly successful. Since one thousand of the probes would weigh no more than the *Spirit* rover, this plan could be a very economical way to explore Mars.

NASA also has high hopes for setting a lander on Europa. The lander would bore through the thick crust of ice, releasing a mobile probe into its vast ocean of liquid water. Exploration of Venus might include a blimp that will be able to navigate through the upper layers of Venus's clouds, sending back data for weeks or even months. NASA might also release balloons or blimps in the atmospheres of Jupiter and Saturn.

The ESA will soon launch its *Solar Orbiter*, which will explore the Sun from a distance closer than any other probe has ever achieved. *Solar Orbiter* will carry its telescopes to just one-fifth of Earth's distance from the Sun, where sunlight will be twenty-five times more intense than on Earth. Meanwhile, Japan has plans to send orbiters to both Venus and Mercury.

Humans will always want to explore strange new places themselves. But space probes will continue to be the trailblazers. They open new paths, seek out new, valuable information, and make amazing new discoveries.

NASA engineers would like to launch a Mars sample-return mission in the future. After a rover gathers samples of the surface, the samples would be put aboard a small rocket, which would then return them to Earth.

GLOSSARY

asteroid: one of the small, rocky celestial bodies that orbit mainly between Mars and Jupiter

asteroid belt: a region of space between Mars and Jupiter where the majority of asteroids orbit

atmosphere: the blanket of gases that surrounds a planet

aurora: the effect of electrically charged particles from the Sun striking the upper atmosphere of Earth

booster: a rocket used to accelerate an object

coma: the cloud of glowing dust and gas surrounding the nucleus of a comet

comet: a small body made up primarily of ice, with dust and rock mixed with it

corona: the outer atmosphere of the Sun

cosmic ray: a stream of radiation of high-penetrating power that originates in outer space. It consists partly of high-energy atomic nuclei.

density: the amount of mass contained within a specific volume

escape velocity: the speed needed to escape the pull of a planet's gravity. Earth's escape velocity is about 7 miles per second (11 km/s).

flyby: a close approach to a planet in which a spacecraft passes very near but does not go into orbit

Kuiper belt: a region of icy bodies orbiting beyond Neptune and Pluto. The belt is named after Gerard Kuiper, the Dutch-American astronomer who first suggested its existence.

lander: a spacecraft designed to land on a planet or moon

launch vehicle: a rocket used to accelerate an object into orbit; also sometimes called a booster

magnetic field: the field of force that surrounds a magnet or another object generating magnetism, such as a planet

magnetometer: an instrument that measures the intensity of a magnetic field

nucleus: the solid core of a comet, usually composed of ice, dust, and rock

orbit: to revolve around; the path a spacecraft follows as it circles a planet; the path a moon or planet follows as it circles a planet or the Sun

orbiter: a spacecraft designed to orbit a moon or planet as a satellite

organic molecule: a molecule containing at least one carbon atom

outgassing: the release of gases from soil or crust of a moon or planet

photometer: an instrument that measures levels of light intensity

probe: any spacecraft designed to visit another planet or moon and send information back to Earth

rover: any spacecraft equipped with wheels that allow it to roam over the surface of a planet or moon

satellite: any small object orbiting a larger one. The Moon is a satellite of Earth.

solar wind: a stream of atoms and atomic particles emitted at high speed from the Sun

space station: a satellite with a human crew

spectrometer: an instrument that determines the chemical makeup of a substance by examining the light it emits or is reflected from it

surface radiation: the amount of radiation from the Sun falling on the surface of a planet or moon

Van Allen belt: two doughnut-shaped regions of radiation surrounding Earth. The belt is named for James Van Allen, who discovered them.

SOURCE NOTES

12–13   NASA, "Apollo 11 Transcripts," Kennedy Space Center, October 20, 2003,
http://www-pao.ksc.nasa.gov/history/apollo/apollo-11/
apollo11transcripts.htm

22   Howard McCurdy, *Faster, Better, Cheaper: Low Cost Innovation in the U.S.
Space Program* (Baltimore: Johns Hopkins University Press, 2001), 117.

SELECTED BIBLIOGRAPHY

Carr, Michael H. *Images of Mars: The Viking Extended Mission NASA SP444*.
Washington, DC: NASA, 1980.

Fimmel, Richard O., Lawrence Colin, and Eric Burgess. *Pioneering Venus: A Planet
Unveiled*. Washington, DC: NASA, 1995.

Fischer, Daniel. *Mission Jupiter: The Spectacular Journey of the Galileo Spacecraft*.
New York: Copernicus Books, 2001.

Gatland, Kenneth. *The Illustrated Encyclopedia of Space Technology*. London: Orion
Books, 1989.

Jet Propulsion Laboratory. *Voyager Encounters Jupiter*. Pasadena, CA: NASA/Jet
Propulsion Laboratory, 1979.

Kraemer, Robert S. *Beyond the Moon: A Golden Age of Planetary Exploration
1971–1978*. Washington, DC: Smithsonian Institution, 2000.

NASA. *Magellan Revealing the Face of Venus JPL400 494*. Pasadena, CA: Jet
Propulsion Laboratory, 1993.

——. *Voyager at Neptune, 1989*. Pasadena, CA: NASA/Jet Propulsion Laboratory,
1989.

FOR FURTHER INFORMATION

Books

Crouch, Tom D. *Aiming for the Stars: The Dreamers and Doers of the Space Age.* Washington, DC: Smithsonian Institution Scholarly Press, 2000.

Elish, Dan. *Satellites*. Salt Lake City: Benchmark Books, 2006.

Fischer, Daniel. *Mission Jupiter: The Spectacular Journey of the Galileo Spacecraft.* New York: Copernicus Books, 2001.

Johnson, Rebecca L. *Satellites*. Minneapolis: Lerner Publications Company, 2006.

Kuhn, Betsy. *The Race for Space: The United States and the Soviet Union Compete for the New Frontier.* Minneapolis: Twenty-First Century Books, 2007.

Miller, Ron. Worlds Beyond series. Minneapolis: Twenty-First Century Books, 2002–2006.

——. *The Grand Tour*. New York: Workman, 2005.

——. *Satellites*. Minneapolis: Twenty-First Century Books, 2008.

——. *Space Exploration*. Minneapolis: Twenty-First Century Books, 2008.

Sherman, Josepha. *Deep Space Observation Satellites*. New York: Rosen, 2003.

Spangenburg, Ray, and Kit Moser. *Wernher Von Braun: Out of the Fire, the Stars.* Danbury, CT: Franklin Watts, 2007.

Vogt, Gregory. *Disasters in Space Exploration*. Minneapolis: Millbrook Press, 2003.

Magazines

Ad Astra
http://www.nss.org/
This is the official magazine of the National Space Society.

Astronomy
http://www.astronomy.com
This magazine keeps up-to-date on current space probes and their discoveries.

Quest
http://www.spacebusiness.com/quest/
This magazine is devoted to space history.

Sky & Telescope
http://skyandtelescope.com
This magazine covers all aspects of astronomy and associated news.

Museums

Adler Planetarium & Astronomy Museum
1300 S. Lake Shore Drive
Chicago, IL 60605
http://adlerplanetarium.com

American Museum of Natural History
Hayden Planetarium
Rose Center for Earth and Space
15 West 81st Street
New York, NY 10024
http://www.amnh.org/

Kansas Cosmosphere and Space Center
1100 N. Plum
Hutchinson, KS 67501
http://www.cosmo.org/visitorinfo/whyhutch.php

Kennedy Space Center
State Road 405
Kennedy Space Center, FL 32899
http://www.kennedyspacecenter.com

Pima Air & Space Museum
6000 E. Valencia Road
Tucson, AZ 85706
http://www.pimaair.org/

San Diego Air & Space Museum
2001 Pan American Plaza
Balboa Park, San Diego, CA 92101
http://www.aerospacemuseum.org/

Smithsonian National Air & Space Museum
6th & Independence SW
Washington, DC 20560
http://www.nasm.si.edu/

U.S. Space and Rocket Center
One Tranquility Base
Huntsville, AL 35805
http://www.spacecamp.com/museum/

Websites

Encyclopedia Astronautica
http://www.astronautix.com/
This website provides an online encyclopedia of spacecraft and space history.

NASA Home Page
http://www.nasa.gov/
The official website of the National Aeronautics and Space Administration provides current mission photos and news.

NASA Office of Policy and Plans
http://www.hq.nasa.gov/office/pao/History/history.html
The official website of NASA's history office provides general information about NASA and links to its other websites.

Planetary Photojournal
http://photojournal.jpl.nasa.gov/index.html
This is the official source for the latest images from all the space probes.

Space.com
http://www.space.com/
This website provides daily news about happenings in space and astronomy.

Space Telescope Science Institute
http://www.stsci.edu/
This is the official website for the Hubble Space Telescope.

Students for the Exploration and Development of Space
http://www.seds.org
This student-based organization promotes the exploration and development of space with programs, publications, membership, and discussion forums.

INDEX

ABOUT THE AUTHOR

Ron Miller is the author and illustrator of about forty books, most of which have been about science, space, and astronomy. His award-winning books include *The Grand Tour* and *The History of Earth*. Among his nonfiction books for young people are *Special Effects*, *The Elements*, and the Worlds Beyond series, which received the 2003 American Institute of Physics Award in Physics and Astronomy. His book, *The Art of Chesley Bonestell*, won the 2002 Hugo Award for Best Non-Fiction. He has also designed space-themed postage stamps and has worked as an illustrator on several science fiction movies, such as *Dune* and *Total Recall*.

PHOTO ACKNOWLEDGMENTS

All images in this book were provided by the author. The following images are used with the permission of: NASA, pp. 1, 4, 6 (both), 8, 10 (all), 11 (left), 14 (both), 15, 17, 18, 19, 20, 21, 24, 26 (both), 27, 30 (both), 31 (both), 34, 36 (all), 40, 42, 44, 45, 47, 48 (both), 49, 50, 51, 52, 53, 54 (all), 56, 59, 60, 61 (both), 62, 63, 64, 65 (both), 66, 67, 68 (all), 69, 70, 71, 72, 73, 74 (both), 76, 77, 78 (both), 80, 82 (center, bottom), 84 (both), 85, 88, 90, 91, 92, 96 (both), 97, 100, 102, 103; courtesy of Jack Coggins, p. 7; Pluto stamp design © 1991 United States Postal Service. All rights reserved. Used with permission, p. 87.

Front Cover: Courtesy of NASA/ JPL-Caltech.